THE LIGHTNING OF POSSIBLE STORMS

ALSO BY JONATHAN BALL

Ex Machina

Clockfire

The Politics of Knives

John Paizs's Crime Wave

Why Poetry Sucks
(co-edited with Ryan Fitzpatrick)

This eBook is otherwise provided to you as-is

The National Gallery

JONATHAN BALL

THE LIGHTNING
OF POSSIBLE
STORMS

Book*hug Press
TORONTO

Library and Archives Canada Cataloguing in Publication

Title: The lightning of possible storms / Jonathan Ball.
Names: Ball, Jonathan, 1979– author.
Identifiers: Canadiana (print) 20200284940 | Canadiana (ebook) 20200284975
  ISBN 9781771666138 (softcover) | ISBN 9781771666145 (EPUB)
  ISBN 9781771666152 (PDF) | ISBN 9781771666169 (Kindle)
Classification: LCC PS8603.A55 L54 2020 | DDC C813/.6—dc23

Printed in Canada

The production of this book was made possible through the generous assistance
of the Canada Council for the Arts and the Ontario Arts Council. Book*hug Press
also acknowledges the support of the Government of Canada through the Canada
Book Fund and the Government of Ontario through the Ontario Book Publishing
Tax Credit and the Ontario Book Fund.

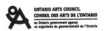

Book*hug Press acknowledges that the land on which we operate is the traditional
territory of many nations, including the Mississaugas of the Credit, the Anishnabeg,
the Chippawa, the Haudenosaunee and the Wendat peoples. We recognize the
enduring presence of many diverse First Nations, Inuit, and Métis peoples and are
grateful for the opportunity to meet and work on this territory.

CONTENTS

National Bestseller / 7

The Best Story Ever Submitted to Your Magazine / 27

Your Letter / 31

Explosions / 43

Costa Rican Green / 77

Judith / 89

The Dark Part of the Sky / 99

George and Gracie / 111

The Nightmare Ballad of the Drunken
Brand Identity with a Cameo by Shakespeare
and a Title That Cannot Get Worse / 123

While You Sleep I Record Your Dreams / 139

Capitalism / 141

The War with the Dead / 153

The Palace of Ice / 159

Narcissus / 167

As We All Should Lie / 171

Wolves in Trains / 177

The Lightning of Possible Storms / 183

About the Author / 191

For Aleya, who will learn why.

I can't help but dream about a kind of criticism that would try not to judge but to bring an oeuvre, a book, a sentence, an idea to life; it would light fires, watch the grass grow, listen to the wind, and catch the sea foam in the breeze and scatter it. It would multiply not judgments but signs of existence; it would summon them, drag them from their sleep. Perhaps it would invent them sometimes—all the better. All the better. Criticism that hands down sentences sends me to sleep; I'd like a criticism of scintillating leaps of the imagination. It would not be sovereign or dressed in red. It would bear the lightning of possible storms.

—Michel Foucault

His glory and his monuments are gone.

—William Butler Yeats

HE ALWAYS WRITES. Aleya places the tea beside his book. She steals a glance (*The Robber* by Robert Walser), careful not to spill because the table shakes (*unstable-table*, she singsongs in thought). The tables all shake because of the warped hardwood floor, but his shakes the worst. Its shaking increases as his pen, held tight enough to whiten his knuckles, jitters across the yellow pad.

His writing is a messy hybrid of cursive and printing. Some words are only half-written, their other halves straight lines, a shorthand of his own design. She can never make anything out.

He doesn't notice her putting down his tea. He never notices her. Aleya doesn't mind, because he always tips her well. In fact, she wishes more of her men would ignore her in this way. So many hit on her or otherwise waste her time with their lonely desperation, the small talk she pretends to find pleasant (though sometimes she doesn't pretend). The women are no better. They display a wider range of attentions, are less predictable in their jealousies, irritations, lusts. The worst customers, of course, whether women or men, are the other writers. Except for him, the writers who come into her tea house take even a glance in their direction as an excuse to escape from their work.

Unlike her other regulars, whose eyes she feels, whose words (however kind) seem too solid, her writer gives Aleya the impression that she means nothing to him. That he'd be just as happy with any other waitress, anybody else as silent and efficient as she. Even the regulars she does like she doesn't like as much as this writer, the one who demands nothing, who seeks only tea and silence. Although this tea house is as chatty as any, Aleya prides herself on keeping the music off during her shifts. During slow periods, the sole noises are the creaking of wood shifting beneath bodies, fingers clicking keys, pens scratching yellow pads.

Her writer scratches his yellow pad, and she wonders, not for the first time, what his name is, whether she might have read anything he's written. He never speaks except to order and he never speaks to anyone else, so she's never caught his name. He never meets anyone here and never runs into anyone he knows. She supposes that is why he comes here, to avoid everyone, to be out in the world and yet practising withdrawal. If he stayed home, he would have to stop writing to make his own tea and wouldn't gain whatever satisfaction he gains from ignoring the world that flows around him.

She fingers her necklace, a thin silver disc she's hammered herself. She watches him write for a moment, watches him ignore her, then slips away.

When she later turns back to him, having served a few more tables, she sees he's slipped away. He always pays when he orders, and often leaves without saying a word, so that in itself does not surprise her. But when she moves to clear his table (another sizable tip, twice the bill), she sees the tea is still warm. Untouched. And a book lies on the table, but not the same book.

She picks it up, peruses the title. *The Lightning of Possible Storms*. She turns it over. There he is, her nameless writer, in the author photo, now named. *Jonathan Ball*. She frowns. Was this part of her tip? She'd been so happy, thinking him oblivious. But he'd left her his book.

She tucks it under one arm and takes it behind the counter, then throws it into a drawer below the till, out of sight. She continues her day, annoyed, lips tight. Her smiles forced and her tips small.

When she closes the tea house, she takes the book out of the drawer again. She supposes she has to read it. He will expect this. Maybe she can have Natalie return it, pretend she'd been the one to clear the table. But, of course, he'd see through that. Aleya always served him, and he always left a large tip. For *her*.

She flips the book open, curious. At least she'll see what he's always writing. Then she spies the dedication.

For Aleya, who will learn why.

Oh no, she thinks. *Oh no.*

She closes the book. She closes her eyes. Maybe this is just a dream. She wishes it a dream, wishes the book away. But even with her eyes closed, feels its dark weight in her hand.

▼

SHE IS GLAD that it is summer, that the walk home is in light. She doesn't fear him, doesn't fear obsession, but she always feels unnerved walking home in winter's dark, and does not want to compound today's unease.

She wonders at the dedication. He's never shown her any attention other than this. Has never spoken to her except to order, always the same words, his private ritual: "Just bring some tea, whatever's good."

Their private ritual, she supposes. After a time, she just started to bring the tea on her first trip to the table, and so he stopped ordering, stopped saying even that much to her. She always brought him something new, judging from the tip what he had liked. He had a taste for sweet teas and for chai. So yes, she supposes they share an intimacy of sorts, however strange. But to waste a dedication on her? He must be so alone.

At home she eats a salad, brews some coffee. Aleya always reads with coffee—tea all day while she works, coffee all night while she reads. Reads. Yes, she'll read the book, read it tonight. She might as well get it over with. The world has changed, and there is no use ignoring the change.

She keeps the house silent. Never much for music or company. When she opened the tea house, her dream had been modest: a business that wouldn't fail, propped up by its location in Calgary's Kensington area. She'd inherited the location from her parents, who'd kept a bookstore. When they died, she closed the failing store, boxed all the books into the basement of the family home she'd also inherited. Took out a second mortgage in order to convert the store into a tea house, with a few baked goods and specialty coffees, some paraphernalia. The irony of all those writers, drafting books in a former bookstore, whose closure served as a comment on their efforts, never escapes her even if it escapes them.

Now another book on top of the boxes in the basement. Always an insomniac, she has been reading a short book every night since she boxed up the store, spreading longer books over a few days or weeks. In this way, she plans to read through the entire bookstore, the sad legacy her parents left.

Her too-young parents, both dead from a gas leak. Dead in this house. While she was away, studying in Winnipeg. In her madness, at the time, she thought she wanted an MBA. She gives the books away once she reads them, never understood why you would read the same book twice. In the three years since she opened the shop, even at this steady pace, she's read through only 713 of the ten thousand books in the basement. Buying not one book in all that time. Another way the gift of the book has disrupted her happy routine.

The coffee's sharpness pleases her and she feels more positive as she settles into her reading chair, a Cleopatra lounger. Worst case, her writer has developed a little crush and she'll have to deflect it, maybe lose a customer and some tips. And the book might not be meant as a love letter—she *has* helped him write it, in a (quite abstract) sense, so perhaps he's just acknowledged something that doesn't require acknowledgement, has overdone things and doesn't mean it the way she is taking it. It would have made more sense to acknowledge her on, say, an *acknowledgements* page (flipping through, she doesn't see one) rather than a dedication, but she supposes this is more poetic, more writerly. Writerlier?

For Aleya, who will learn why.

Who will learn why.

The phrase unnerves her more than the dedication itself. If the *why* isn't because she serves him so well whenever he comes into the tea house to write, then why?

If it *is* a love letter, this book, how she deals with it will depend on its extent. If the book is too warm, she will be cold, will send Natalie to serve him the next time he comes in. He'll get the message.

So Aleya opens the book and begins to read, wondering why.

NATIONAL BESTSELLER

IT'S ABOUT TIME I made some fucking money. That's what Jonathan was thinking when he decided to write a national bestseller. If he was thinking straight, he would have decided to write an international bestseller. But he was Canadian and Canadians dream small.

It's about time I made some fucking money, Jonathan repeated to his agent.

She agreed. And how, Meerkat asked, do you intend to do that?

I'm going to write a National Bestseller. (Already there were capital letters.)

Good luck.

I'm serious. His spastic fingers, the hands that always shook (a genetic defect, *benign sporadic tremor*) popped open his briefcase and rummaged out a copy of the latest *Quill & Quire*. He flipped to the bestseller lists. His fingers tremored in their sporadic way (yet so benign!) and he almost dropped the magazine.

When did you get a briefcase?

It's all part of the package. (There was a package now.) Every time I see these bestseller lists, I notice my name's not there. And look at these books. Garbage. I tried to read through one of these lists last month. Gah. It's not that they're unimaginative, formulaic. They're not readable.

That's your opinion. And we know how valuable your opinion is on the free market. Besides, people don't need to read them, just buy them.

Exactly. It has very little to do with the actual writing. Everything depends on other factors: the marketing budget, the plot hook, some failed novelist-turned-reviewer. Who's hip, who's young, who spent a year in Afghanistan, who looks good in a muscle shirt. Who's sleeping with Margaret Atwood.

You sound paranoid. Like a bitter amateur. So what's your plan? Seduce Peggy?

She grinned over her drink. She thought it was oh-so-funny. Jonathan didn't laugh. Lisa Meerkat was the worst agent ever. She even had a stupid name. Sometimes he thought he'd be better off without an agent. He'd be better off without Meerkat and in Toronto, centre of publishing, centre of the universe.

He didn't know how Meerkat managed to make all those sales. All those big sales for other people, but did she ever make a big sale for him? No. But Caleb, she got Caleb all the money in the world. She wouldn't confirm it, but Jonathan heard she got Caleb six figures for his first novel. The novel Jonathan edited.

Oh, before I forget—stay away from Caleb Zimmerman.

What?

You know what I mean. Quit pestering him.

What pestering? I've been helping him with his novel.

Quit helping.

He's my friend. You've got to help out your friends. He's new to this whole publishing racket.

He's my client now.

On my recommendation.

I'll watch his back, don't worry.

I'm your client too.

And I love you just as much as I love Caleb. Only different.

You sound like my mom.

▼

HALFWAY THROUGH THE MEETING, he decided to take a loss. He wouldn't even tell her about his plan. Dropped the topic after she began talking about Caleb. He thought she would be excited about his plan, but she only wanted to talk about Caleb.

To be fair, she didn't say anything else about Caleb. But his ego had taken the blow. He wondered if she remembered how his first novel sung to her from the slush pile. One sentence and she fell in love, faxed him a contract, and had him signed to her agency before she got to the fiftieth page. He wondered if she remembered.

Do I remember? Of course, I remember. How could I forget? On page fifty, the main character died and never returned.

It's never been done before.

Yeah, well. It'll never be done again.

The book (*Forever Ends a Day*) wasn't well-reviewed, but so what? It had its following. After it came out, he'd stumbled across a Facebook site where people could "become a fan" of Jonathan Ball. There were ninety-nine fans. He became number one hundred.

Now, your second novel, that's when you really proved you had the goods. Jonathan's second novel was about a gun nut who decided to live in the BC rainforests, Walden-like, and ended up trying to teach animals the ways of civilization. (One reviewer called it "the Canadian answer to *Penguin*

Island," which he had to look up, but on the basis of the Wikipedia summary he agreed.) The culmination of the gun nut's project was his attempt to construct an effective militia from the local bear population.

The novel had been hailed as a comic masterpiece, and he was nominated for a lot of awards. He sweated, terrified, through every ceremony, trying to decide which would be worse: winning or losing. He lost. And in the moment, he was almost happy. Almost. The novel wasn't supposed to be funny.

For his third book, *The Negative Blooms*, he collected his short stories. The National Bestseller would be his fourth. Even all those award nominations hadn't made *The Right to Arm Bears* a National Bestseller. He didn't know what you had to do to get a National Bestseller around here, but he would find out.

▼

EVERYONE AGREED THAT Jonathan was a great writer. They just didn't want to read anything he wrote.

You're such a great writer! Jana sighed. I wish I could write as well as you. But no, I haven't finished your book yet. I heard it was nominated for an award, though! That must be great.

It didn't win.

Oh.

He never won. Well, that wasn't true. There was the time he got that free hot dog, in Grade 4. He guessed forty-two and he was right.

You're so smart. I just didn't understand the book.

What didn't you understand?

Oh, you know. Jana gave a vague wave, like she was swatting a fly in slow-motion. She breathed in, long and loud, like it just took all her strength to kill that imaginary fly, the simile-fly. It's just too deep for me. When she breathed in like that, long and loud, a reverse sigh, her perfect breasts strained up and away, up and away, up toward him then away, away, away. I started reading the new Dan Brown instead. But it's good, your book, I mean, the writing is so fantastic, and it's all just so smart.

He would never sleep with Jana.

Maybe you should use quotation marks, said Caleb. People like quotation marks.

"Fuck you."

"See?"

Caleb was just trying to help. It wasn't his fault that everyone loved him like they loved Jesus. He had 3,764 fans on Facebook already with his first novel not even published yet. Caleb had a website at www.calebzimmerman.com where people could look at the cover of the not-yet-published book and masturbate if they wanted, or read the first chapter, which 3,764 people had done. Jonathan was thinking he might get a blog one of these days.

▼

NOT DAUNTED BY COMMON SENSE (what writer was?), he drank five cups of coffee and his fingers skipped over his keyboard. This was going to be easy! In two hours, he had almost ten pages. If he kept up this pace he could have a full novel, three hundred solid pages, in two and a half days. Why not stay up all night! Before the weekend was out, before he had to return to his job teaching literature to students who didn't like books, he would be a bestselling-novelist-in-embryo.

He pressed on to page twelve before skipping back, to check a plot point, see what he had written. It was just a bunch of gibberish. The plot made no sense at all, just meandered into endless corners.

Would anybody put up with this nonsense? They seemed to like Thomas Pynchon. But Pynchon had method, was rigorous even, below his madcap surfaces. He wondered how many books Thomas Pynchon sold. Enough to live a reclusive life of writing. But who knew, maybe Pynchon was a schoolteacher somewhere. Maybe he held the patent to some bizarre invention. He couldn't remember seeing Pynchon on the bestseller lists.

He shuffled his feet through the pile of empty coffee cups. Maybe he was drinking too much coffee? Or too little? There was something to be said for writing so much, good or bad. He could always transform some of it, maybe most of it, into useable material in the second draft. Was this why so many novelists had (or used to have, before it stopped being sexy) coke habits? Stephen King wrote a lot of best-sellers with a coke habit. But wrote even more without one, Jonathan supposed.

Anyway, he could barely afford all this coffee, never mind cocaine. How did authors afford coke habits? And he maintained a childish aversion to drugs, which would turn you into a gun-toting madman without fail. But cocaine aside, maybe there was something to this line of thought. Maybe there was something common to bestselling, or at least successful, writers—something they shared.

He skimmed some biographies online, and as far as he could tell the single thing successful writers had in common was that they didn't die, and didn't quit writing. With few exceptions, they were folks who worked hard for a long time and succeeded by virtue of the sole fact that they stuck around until they were no longer ignored.

Was there anything to learn from this? He hoped not. Otherwise his whole "plan" was a waste of time. He couldn't let himself be distracted by the biographies of authors who lived in different times anyway. The circumstances of their lives did not apply to this new market scenario.

Back to the original scheme, of harvesting the bestseller lists for ideas he could combine in fire-hot fiction.

He pored through list after list, from back issues of the *New York Times*, *Publishers Weekly*, and *Quill & Quire*— he'd first subscribed to the latter two for the book reviews but later renewed them for the industry news. Who sold what where. As if any of it might make any difference in his life.

After rereading his notes on two years of bestseller lists, he'd compiled a list of his own:

THINGS PEOPLE SEEM TO LIKE INSIDE OF BOOKS
- *vampires*
- *mysteries*
- *coded messages about treasure or mysteries*
- *eating healthy (reading about it, anyway)*
- *exercising (ditto)*
- *sex (creepy, unsexy sex)*
- *cute kids*
- *the power of positive thinking*
- *wizards*
- *cute kids who are wizards*
- *animals, cute*
- *quantum mechanics (new age nonsense about)*
- *Jesus*
- *coded messages about Jesus*
- *how Jesus invented quantum mechanics*

It was a demoralizing exercise. What did he care about vampires? What did he know about positive thinking? He wasn't a code-breaker or quantum physicist. He didn't understand why anyone would allow a pet inside the house.

Desperate times called, so he sat still and thought of kindness for five whole minutes, but Jesus refused to shine light into his life.

What he was going to do with this list he did not know.

He retreated to steady ground. And redrafted those twelve pages of plotless gibberish into pseudo-autobiographical gibberish. Something playful and truthful in the story now, at least. He'd show it to Meerkat. Not much, but a start, in some direction. He wondered what Meerkat would say.

▼

MEERKAT LIVED UP to her name for once, pounced. I can't sell this book.

What?!!! Why the fuck not?

Well, for starters, there's too much swearing. And too many exclamation marks.

That's how it needs to be!!! The tone is tied to the character, even though it's written in the third person, and the character is frustrated, his life is typified by frustration, so he needs to swear. And exclaim.

I get it, it just sucks. And another thing. Put some quotation marks in.

"Absolutely not."

"Jon, I'm dying here, trying to figure out what I could do with this, where I could go."

"You're asking me to dumb it down, to pander to the masses."

"I thought the whole point of this was to pander to the masses?"

Touché.

"So take out all the French. And that accent in the word Montreal. It's bad enough you mention Montreal in the first place. At least you didn't mention your beloved Winnipeg."

"Now I'm the one who's dying."

"You said you wanted this book to become a National Bestseller. I'm just trying to help. The other thing is, your settings are too vague, it's like they're non-existent. I mean, when people are talking I can't even tell if they're face to face or on the phone, for the most part."

Before he could respond, the barista interrupted to take their order. She was a slip of a girl with short purple bangs and a slight upturn to the right of her mouth. Jonathan had hoped Jana would be working, but oh well.

He ordered a chai latte and Meerkat ordered one too—they had this in common at least. While Meerkat flirted with the barista girl he edged his chair back, tipped a little, felt his senses rush with the stimulus of the coffee shop. The air hummed with wireless Internet and mid-morning conversations. The rich smell of a hundred blends soaked out of the floor. He slipped off a shoe to run his foot over the rough, aged boards.

It was all very evocative.

"And quit being so clever."

"But I *am* clever."

"Don't whine."

"Let me just look over my notes here, so I can make sure we're on the same page." He made a show of hoisting an imaginary notebook and flipping back a few imaginary pages. "You want me to gut the character and the tone to make the story blander, and use unnecessary quotation marks for no earthly reason. Also, I should remove any specific references to geography while making the settings more evocative. And you want me to make the story less playful and less fun, with less jokes. In general, I should write like I'm trying to explain to a five-year-old how to tie his shoes. Language that's plain and straightforward, totally neutered."

"Please don't use the word *neutered*. No mutilating genitals, or—well, unless you want to make it *all* genitals or *all* mutilation, we could get you a pseudonym and go after the genre markets—"

"I think I understand."

▼

BUT HE DIDN'T UNDERSTAND. Desperate, he decided to talk to Caleb.

Since receiving his fancy advance, Caleb spent every morning at the same coffeeshop. Café Carné was a hipster joint that boasted coffee-infused beef products. Jonathan had discovered it and introduced it to Caleb, who fell in love with their coffee-infused Mongolian beef noodle dish. He had started a habit of going to the coffeeshop to write and rewarding himself for hitting his 1,000-word target with lunch. If he didn't make the target then he left without lunch. The system worked, and Caleb ended up dedicating his manuscript to Café Carné.

When Jonathan arrived, he spied Caleb in the corner, headphones on, typing while his coffee and a coffee-infused meat bun snuggled up against some book. Caleb clicked his pointer fingers across his laptop, chicken-pecking out more pages. Jonathan *tsked* at the poor keyboarding. When he was in school, the teachers would smash his knuckles with a wooden ruler if they caught him doing something like that.

He sauntered over to Caleb and sat down across from him, picking up the book, a worn copy of *Art & Fear* by David

Bayles & Ted Orland. Jonathan had given the book to Caleb as a housewarming gift when he moved into his condo.

Caleb slipped his headphones down as Jonathan perused the book. "Hey, nice to see you, been a while."

"Yeah, I've been busy. Working on a new book."

"Hey, I know what that's like." Caleb gestured to his laptop and took a bite out of the meat bun.

"Wanted to talk to you about the new book actually, so that's why I came down here. I've been stuck."

"Cool, yeah, sure thing. I just gotta finish up, I'm doing 2,000 words a day now and I'm only at, uh"—he glanced down—"1,138."

"Like George Lucas."

Caleb offered a puzzled look that suggested he didn't get the reference. Jonathan refused to explain any reference he made, as a general principle, so they passed an awkward moment in silence.

Caleb chomped the meat bun to end the standoff. "So yeah, hang out a bit, I should be done in like an hour. Two max." Then he popped his headphones back on and went back to chicken-pecking.

Jonathan just sat there. Staring.

While Caleb worked.

He began to feel uncomfortable. The waiter came by and asked what he wanted and he ordered his own meat bun and some sort of latte with bouillon.

Maybe he would write after all. But the whole problem was he didn't know what to write. He pulled out his laptop, figuring he would at least make a show of working. He fired it up and signed onto the café Wi-Fi while the waiter delivered his order.

Fucking Caleb. Jonathan was the one who got him writing in this coffeeshop in the first place. When they were both focused on writing their master's thesis projects, they made a deal to meet every morning to have an excuse to get out of bed and out the door at a time in their lives when, coasting on scholarships with their time otherwise unstructured, they separately found themselves too often still in pyjamas in the afternoon. Fed up with their lack of productivity, they decided on a system where they woke, travelled to meet at Café Carné, reviewed their plans for the day over coffee, and then ignored each other (just like Caleb was ignoring him now) and dived into their work. Jonathan stopped this when his thesis (which became his first novel) was completed, but Caleb kept at it, taking a later shift at his bookstore job, which meant reducing his hours, to stick with his morning writing routine. It paid off when he got his advance, although he probably gobbled half that up in coffee-kebabs over the years.

He watched Caleb, whose gaze only left his laptop screen when he lost his place chicken-pecking the keyboard. People seemed to like Caleb. He liked Caleb too, of course, but not as much as other people did. Maybe he should just write about Caleb.

Why the hell not? Caleb could be the main character of his novel. He'd introduced Caleb to Meerkat, who'd gotten him that big ole deal. Caleb owed him.

▼

CALEB ZIMMERMAN WAS asleep and dreaming dreams of sexy Japanese girls, but they were only interested in trying to sell him photographs of the CN Tower. "It's the tallest free-standing structure in the world," they cooed, batting false lashes and showing their eyeteeth when they smiled. "But not for long."

Firm legs trailed down from tan miniskirts. The girls were all different, but wore odd uniforms that were half schoolgirl outfit and half tourist attraction worker, and cute black slipper-shoes with ankle socks. The socks were blue as sky, with little grey CN Towers pointing up to taut calves and beyond.

The photographs were not postcards but large, framed portraits. The smallest was a foot tall and the largest must have been ten. It lay on its side, held in the air between two girls, the tower's spire pointing straight at the smaller girl's larger breasts. The girl winked at Caleb.

"This would look great in your bedroom, wouldn't it?" said the smaller girl. A short pink tie dangled from her neck down between her thick breasts and she readjusted her hands to place one underneath the tower's head/observation deck. Caleb admitted that it all would look excellent in his bedroom. The girl tilted her head and her smile got warmer. "Maybe we could wrap it up for you?"

"It's not cheap," the other girl broke in, "but it's a Collector's Item." Caleb could hear the capital letters. This girl held the tower's base and was a good foot taller than the other girl, just a few inches taller than Caleb, who told people he was five-ten but had never bothered to measure himself.

The taller girl wore a blue tie. They were in a large white room, but Caleb wasn't sure where. The girls filled the room, dressed the same but with different-coloured ties and holding different framed photos of the tower. Blue Tie waved her hand to re-indicate the tower, in case Caleb had somehow forgotten about it. "Of course, the photo will increase in value. It comes with a Certificate of Authenticity, which also confirms the date on which the photo was taken, and that on this date the CN Tower was still the tallest free-standing structure in the world."

"It's signed by the Prime Minister," said Pink Tie in a husky croon. "The Certificate, I mean."

A girl in a green tie holding a mid-sized photo of the tower at night spoke up. "All of the photographs come with Certificates, and all are guaranteed to be of the CN *Tower when it was still the tallest free-standing structure in the world."*

Caleb wanted to look at the girls but they always caught him looking and redirected his gaze to the photographs, which were nice but less attractive than the girls. He didn't want to buy a photograph of the CN *Tower, even if it came with a Certificate and was guaranteed to increase in value, because he didn't want to become a collector. Buy one photo of the* CN *Tower and soon you'd have to buy them all. He knew people who collected things and considered it an obsessive, expensive waste of time.*

But he didn't know how to say this without breaking the hearts of hundreds of sexy Japanese girls. So instead he said, "But the CN *Tower is the world's tallest free-standing structure."*

"Not for long," said Blue Tie. "The Emirates is building Burj Dubai, planned for completion in 2009. Although its final height is a secret, it is certain to take the world record away from Toronto's CN *Tower. Therefore, now is the best time to buy these photos, because soon they will exponentially increase in value."*

As if to underscore the statement, the opening riff from Nirvana's "Smells Like Teen Spirit" erupted, startling Caleb and saleswomen alike. It was like a musical sonic boom.

"Burj Dubai?"

Another guitar riff exploded into the air.

▼

"I DON'T KNOW that I'm comfortable with all that *sexy girl* stuff. Maybe take my name out of this story."

"Yeah sure, whatever, but like, what do you think of it otherwise?"

Caleb didn't quite know what to think. "Where are the guitar riffs coming from?"

"I don't know, it just needed something. Some sort of shift to signal that the scene was concluding."

"Doesn't make much sense."

"It's a dream."

"Maybe his roommate is practising guitar, and the guitar wakes him up?"

"Maybe."

Caleb reread the ending of the scene and chuckled. "You just put in a massive, world-shaking guitar riff for no logical reason, because you wanted a shift in tone? Man, your process is wild."

"I want to know about *your* process." Jonathan closed the laptop, almost squishing Caleb's stupid fingers (he was in the middle of fixing a spelling mistake, couldn't help himself). "I keep getting stuck in the plot. What do you do when you get stuck?"

Caleb scratched his head. "I mean, I don't really get stuck. Because I'm working from an outline. You know, like you taught me."

"Well sure, I mean I get that I taught you to do stuff like that but you're at the point where you're doing better than me. You must have some wisdom to impart."

"Doing better than you?"

"You've got that big advance now."

Caleb waved the comment away while he stuffed some Mongolian coffee-beef into his mouth. Did they have coffee in ancient Mongolia? And if they did, did they feed it to their cows, or marinade beef slabs in it, or whatever it was these hipster chefs did during working hours? Was it still correct to call this monstrosity Mongolian beef?

Caleb wiped his mouth. "I mean, whatever, the advance is nice but that's all market stuff, you can't pay attention to any of that stuff. It comes, it goes, it's a wave, you're just somewhere in the water and it hoists you up or knocks you down, whatever."

"You just gotta swim, huh?"

"Yeah. I mean, that's what you told me." Caleb shrugged and slurped a noodle. "I don't get that marketing stuff. That's why I've got Meerkat. And the publishers, and whatever. That's their deal. I mean, I learned some of it just to learn some of it, so I could help them out, but I only work on that stuff when I have free time. I've got to focus on writing. That's my job."

They were quiet a moment, eating.

Then Caleb laughed. "Dude, I don't know what you want to ask me. I'm just doing all the stuff you told me to do, and it's working out great!"

Jonathan stuck his fork through a strip of coffee-beef. What a stupid fucking idea, coffee-beef. What a waste of fucking time.

▼

LATER ON, WHILE HE WAS on his phone scrolling through Facebook, he spied an ad for an online course company called Masterclass. They were advertising a course by Dan Brown. It had a thirty-day refund policy. He clicked through and bought it right away.

The Dan Brown Masterclass consisted of nineteen videos. He skimmed the titles and clicked on number eighteen, "Life as a Writer." The mini-description read, "Dan explains the importance of persistence, shares tips on how to build a team that believes in you, and teaches you how to write a query letter that will stand out in agency slush piles." All things he figured he could learn from Dan Brown.

Brown started by telling a story about sitting in a bookstore at a signing table after his first book had been published. Nobody came to his table. Finally, just as he was thinking he should pack up, Brown and a customer locked eyes. She beelined toward him. He smiled a massive smile.

She asked if he could point her to the bathroom.

Brown chuckled, remembering the pain.

"And at that moment, I felt as low as I could possibly feel as a writer. Here I had just spent almost two years writing this book, and really nobody wanted to talk to me about it, nobody wanted to buy it. And what I learned from that moment was that the process itself needs to be the reward."

Brown went on to explain how his first three books had failed. However, retroactively, with the success of *The Da Vinci Code*, they became popular and now are thought of as big hits. Brown then detailed how during the five years in between his first book being published and *The Da Vinci Code* becoming a bestseller, he spent a massive amount of time and energy promoting his own books, managing to sell just enough copies that his publisher wanted the next book, although not enough copies to have a self-sustaining career.

Brown just kept focusing on selling a little more, a little more, until finally he reached a combination of hitting a tipping point with his work and having a bit of luck with his writing. Brown then noted, as Caleb had, about how a writer needed to surround himself with other people—publishers, agents, and booksellers—who are also invested in his success. Without the slow build of the previous books, Brown would never have been in the position for a publisher to justify the kind of marketing that made a success like *The Da Vinci Code* possible.

Jonathan looked over his notes.

First, Dan Brown had to relearn that the focus should be on the writing, not on career success. All the things Caleb had just told him, the things he had previously told Caleb, Brown was now telling him too.

Second, Brown had to spend real time and money—his own time, his own money—doing everything he could to try to sell books. He bought an ad pushing himself as a talk show guest and booked himself discussing what he'd learned from researching the book, borrowed a car (since his was broken), and drove to rotary clubs trying to sell books out of the trunk, and so on.

Third, he kept writing books. When one failed, he wrote another. Just like Meerkat said he should. Eventually, reading the galleys for *The Da Vinci Code*, Brown said to himself that he had finally done it—but not necessarily in a happy way. He worried he had done his best work and it wouldn't matter. "This is the novel I would want to read. Here it is. This has everything in it that I as a reader would want. And if this doesn't work, then maybe I shouldn't be a writer, because nobody shares my taste." Lucky for Brown, others did.

Jonathan flipped through his notes. More of the same.

- *Books don't become bestsellers by themselves.*
- *One single book won't make your career.*

What a load of shit.

There had to be a shortcut. There had to be a way.

▼

HE HAD STARTED to have dangerous thoughts. *Maybe I can do this, but do it right. Maybe I can write a calculated, cynical novel that is still good.*

He couldn't. Nobody could. All those idiots on the bestseller lists, those horrible writers with their horrible books, they *believed* (as did the good writers on the bestseller lists, the ones he refused to acknowledge). They believed in their work. And their agents and their publishers believed in them, and so did their readers.

Those horrible writers were honest, scrupulous hacks. No one set out to write or publish a bad book, like he planned to do, and even he couldn't seem to do it. Oh, he might write a bad book, like he'd written bad books in the past. But he would only write a bad book after trying to write a good one. He wouldn't have the energy to finish otherwise, and if some miracle lent him that strength, and he did finish, it would not be convincing. You would be able to smell his lack of effort, his lack of interest. It would lift right off the page in an acrid cloud.

The truth came at him, barrelled out of a depressing gun. He dodged. He weaved. He zigged and zagged, and for the moment avoided it, but the shots would continue to fire, would connect with him one day. But in the meantime, he'd zig and zag, try to hammer out a work of genius. Maybe it was possible, if he only held fast to his delusion.

He was going to write a National Bestseller.

THE BEST STORY EVER
SUBMITTED TO YOUR MAGAZINE

THIS LETTER CONCERNS the best story ever submitted to your magazine. I shall submit this story at a later date. Meanwhile, I write to prepare you for the submission, which shall come unbidden, in a private moment, after devastation.

Your eyes will circle the room, restless to keep dry, and fall upon the manuscript. Some word spied on that first page shall be the perfect word for that moment. It shall compel you to read on, and this reading will change your life forever.

For this reason, I shall ignore your guidelines and will not enclose a title page or cover letter with my submission. The manuscript shall arrive in your office unnoticed. It will not be there, and then, without further warning, it *will* be there. Perhaps slipped into your slush pile by some intern who skimmed the story and saw its promise, but did not read it— not in the way *you* shall read it—and so did not recognize it as, in fact, the best story ever submitted to your magazine.

I cannot say much about the particular content of the story, which makes it difficult to describe. Anything I tell you about the story now will defuse the surprise of your first reading, and it is this first reading that shall change your life. Subsequent readings will deepen your appreciation of the story's complexities, each bringing you back to the story as to a lover's body. But this first reading shall remain magical, the primal reason for your love.

Another reason I cannot divulge the particular content of the story is this: I do not yet know what this story shall contain. I wait, monkish, for revelation. You might question my confidence then, but I question yours. How is it that you have lost hope?

You should trust. Trust that the best wine is yet to be drunk, the best story yet to be submitted.

I shall send you this story, you of all readers, in part *because* you have lost hope. In so many ways, in such small ways. Countless miniature losses not yet collated into crisis. This story shall be written for you. It shall transcend the occasion of *you*, to say something to others, but you shall remain its first reader—its true reader—and so, in a paradox, will hesitate to publish this story.

It shall speak to you with such gravity, such precision, that you will think your reaction a mere personal tic. You will not trust your judgment. You will hold the story close, keep it at hand.

With each new reading you will become more convinced of its beauty and power, yet devise new reasons to delay publication. Not able to bear the thought of rejecting the story, neither will you be able to bear the thought of accepting it, publishing it—sharing it with others, letting it go free. You will keep it on hand longer than is decent.

I know this, and I understand. I shall not await your response, nor shall I submit the story elsewhere. We accept even the impossible, given time.

Perhaps that same industrious intern, the one angling for your job, will rifle through your office. She will pick the story up off your desk, where it sits dog-eared, and read it again, give it a *real* read. Perhaps your receipt of the submission will be tracked by others somehow, and demands for your verdict made. In any case, you shall find yourself forced to proclaim the only thing that you can proclaim: *Yes, it should be published.*

Yes.

All your reasons against the story shall fall away, all those illusions you built up to protect it from the world, to protect yourself. They shall fall away, and you shall publish the story.

You need not contact me regarding the story, only publish it. Yes, the rights are available. I refuse payment. No, you know that those edits are superfluous. If it were a different story, another story, then we might talk. I would be happy to talk. But this story is different—you know this as well as I do. This story is something else, perfect, a jewel.

In the final accounting, it is not my story, not yours. It just passed through our lives to transform them in its passing. And it shall continue to pass, from the pages of your magazine to anthologies, to new readers. In living its own life, the story shall lay its inky hands on countless others, marking them, healing. In small, immeasurable ways it shall alter this world.

It shall refine its readers like a purifying fire. It shall be a catalyst, the moment that is necessary. It shall dazzle all, this story. Wind its way into every small life. Find us dying in houses with too many rooms.

I do not know how I will ever write this story. But I am trying, and trust that I will.

If I never die. If the world does not die.

It shall be the best story ever submitted to your magazine.

YOUR LETTER

Dear ——

October 27

Thank you for your letter.

I received it yesterday. A pleasant surprise, to say the least. I hadn't expected to hear from you again at all, never mind so soon.

Is it soon? It seems soon.

I knew it was from you once I saw my name. Isn't that funny? It was *my* name, not yours, that let me know who the letter was from. How you wrote my name. *James*, your *s* trailing, as if straining to leave.

You always called me James—even my parents call me Jim, but you always called me James, because you knew it was what I preferred. Even though everybody calls me Jim and I don't complain.

It's sitting on my end table now. It smells like you. Your perfume, I mean. I hope that doesn't sound strange. I only say it because you mix your own perfume and so of course you smell unique. You do so many things yourself. I have always admired that.

Your handwriting is beautiful. I would have recognized it anyway, even if you had written *Jim*. Those long, thin letters. Reaching upwards, reaching out.

Thank you for your letter. Should I read it? I haven't read it. It's not that I am afraid.

It's that I like this. Not knowing what it says, what gift you've given me.

What words. Those long, gossamer strands.

October 28

It will be my birthday soon. It must be a card. It feels so thick, so firm.

Not a letter at all then.

But maybe. Inside.

That smell.

October 29

Thinking tonight. Remembering that party at Gwen's house, where I first met your friends. I felt like a zoo animal, on display and aware. Under inspection.

I seemed to pass muster. After some initial discomfort, preliminary grilling from Gwen and your closer circle, I was let loose, while they conferred with one another and passed judgments.

I found you by the punch bowl, looking sad, and asked what was wrong. You said you didn't know many of the people there, which I thought strange. But then I realized that most of your friends were in the kitchen, talking about me.

I didn't like you being so ill-at-ease, so I taught you a game I play to make myself comfortable when I don't know anybody at a party. You pick out and imagine what people are like based on their shirts. Then you match people romantically based on these assumed interests. After that the game becomes matchmaker, where you consider it your duty to bring these couples together, and to this end start talking to one while looking for opportunities to bring the other into the conversation. Then you have a purpose, a goal—you always know where you want to drive the conversation and it becomes less of a struggle to talk to somebody new.

You thought this silly and neurotic, but we matched shirts together anyway. While doing this your friends poured out of the kitchen and into the party, led by Gwen, who made a beeline for us and told you I seemed like quite a catch. Which was a comment meant for me, to let me know I had been deemed suitable, at least until further notice.

After that the night was nice but not memorable—in the way that parties, although fun, often blend together unless something particular stands out. And then only those particulars get remembered.

I remember you standing beside that punch bowl. After my examination in the kitchen, it was a relief to see you again. But you looked so alone. You were wearing your grey dress, the one that would look drab on anybody else but looks elegant on you. You had your hair down, straightened for the occasion. The only other times I remember you straightening your hair were the day I took you to my sister's wedding and the night of our first date, when you looked so different with your straight hair that I thought for a moment I had the wrong apartment. At the party you wore your hair down so that it hung just over your eyes, almost covering them. Your beautiful eyes.

You held your glass of punch before you like it was something that could protect you and you held your right elbow in your left hand as if cold. I felt so terrible for leaving you alone. But then you saw me and you smiled and gave a timid wave and I was struck by how different you looked when you smiled, and it made me wish you smiled more often.

October 30

I want to tell you something. It doesn't matter what your letter says. Things won't change. I will still love you and it will still mean nothing.

I don't mean to sound accusatory, or make you uncomfortable. I'm just trying to be honest. I know I haven't always been honest. And I've always appreciated your honesty in the past. In the long run. Maybe not all the time, not at the time, but later, upon reflection.

So it doesn't matter. Whatever you've written. I will appreciate the gesture. I am happy to remain in your thoughts. I think about you a lot. It's not that I want you back. Well, of course I want that, but that's not what I mean. I'm glad we didn't keep on the way we were. I don't want that back. I'd like to recapture what we had before. But it's not possible, I know that, so my thinking about it is just a vague regret. I wish things had worked out, or at least worked out better. It's sad to be surprised by your letter.

Letters. I am always writing letters. Letters I never send. Letters I send and regret. Letters to myself. The occasional love letter.

You wrote me three letters the entire time we were going out. Three letters for the hundreds I wrote you. Four, I suppose, now. I kept them all. They are in the bedroom closet, on the overhead shelf.

Do you still have any of the letters I sent you? I wrote so many. I would be surprised if you kept them.

I love your letters. I loved them, I mean. Well, I still love them, but I don't read them anymore. I just keep them on the shelf. I don't even think about them, not really, it's just that receiving your letter reminded me of those three old ones. I still love them even though I don't read them or think about them anymore. You know what I mean.

I'm sorry for getting so upset. You couldn't help things. They change. And I was so difficult. Depressed all the time. It was a bad time in my life, and yours too. We were both so unhappy. Forced to settle. I wanted to be a novelist—I *still* want to be a novelist—but was stuck writing copy for the neighbourhood section of the paper, fluff articles that weren't even distributed in some parts of the city. You still dreamt of joining an orchestra but weren't able to practise between your two waitressing jobs. I told you to bring your violin to my place, that you shouldn't have to lose your practice time because of me, that I would love to hear you play. Or maybe we didn't have to see each other so often, maybe you needed more time for yourself, for your work. You asked why I didn't want to see you.

That's not what I meant, I said, I was just trying to be supportive. You didn't say anything but I knew you thought I was back-pedalling, that really I wished you would come over less often. Which was not what I meant, not at all.

We had so many arguments like that. Sometimes I didn't even know what our arguments were about. Something I said taken the wrong way or me picking a fight when I was frustrated at other things in my life. Or you picking a fight, but then you would never tell me what the fight was about, why you were angry. You always insisted you weren't angry, even when you refused to speak to me except to pick a fight, as if you knew nothing but fighting.

I often think of our final fight, when you said you didn't love me anymore and I asked what had changed and you said nothing had changed and I said I didn't understand and you said you didn't understand either and you looked like you were going to cry but you never cried.

I forget what else we said then. I hope I didn't hurt your feelings, but I must have. I know I tried. Anyway, I want you to know that I don't hold anything against you. I guess I should've told you this before.

I can't believe you wrote to me first. You, who never wrote. Things are better now. I'm better now. The worst is over. I'm okay. I want you to know that I'm okay. I still care for you but I'm not taking your letter as a sign that you want to try again or anything. I'm just taking it for what it is, a letter. Nothing more.

Maybe that sounds a little silly, considering I haven't read it yet. But I know you and I know it'll just be a nice, polite, normal letter that says *hi* and *how's it going* and that you are writing just to say you still care about me though not in the same way, and maybe we can be friends. I'd like to be friends. I know you aren't writing because you want more than that and I just mean to say that I'm not sitting around moping and wishing we could be more than friends again.

I sound so awkward. I'm just trying to be polite. I don't mean to sound strange. It doesn't matter anyway. This is just one of those letters I'm writing for myself that I won't send. I do this all the time. You know me.

I guess I wouldn't blame you if you didn't keep them. How could I expect you to keep them? Even if you loved them. There were so many.

October 31
Everywhere, masks.

November 1

I'm feeling better today. It was a real shock to get your letter. I'll try to explain. When things ended I was a wreck. You know this. But what you don't know is that after we stopped talking, after I got over feeling sorry for myself, I did a lot of thinking and came to realize that you were right. Things were wonderful, and then they stopped being wonderful. There's no point in trying to pin blame. I can't think of any reason why things didn't work out. There was no reason. It was just the case.

I suppose I should tell you how things are now. With me. Well, work is the same in most ways but I have started to look at it another way. I am still doing the same stories, but I have begun to look at these as more than disposable fluff pieces. I've come to feel that it is important, in a world that can be so isolating, to have a sense of community. It's important to read about yourself and people like you, to feel that the things you do matter somehow, to someone, if only in small ways.

I remember the first time I read a novel set in Winnipeg, one that wasn't set in Toronto or New York or somewhere else. I remember recognizing the landmarks and looking at my city differently after that, as not just a place to escape from but as a place where it was possible to live. I think that was the first time I wanted to be a writer, or, rather, the first time I felt I *could* be a writer, that being born outside of Toronto or New York didn't mean I was doomed to a life without meaning. So I've started looking at my job differently. I'm not saving lives but I'm making people feel a bit bigger in a world that makes them feel small.

I've also been doing a lot of work on my novel, working steadily, not stopping and starting and rewriting endlessly like you'd remember. I scrapped it and began again, as I have a habit of doing, but for the last time. I'm almost done now. Of late, I've been living a rather solitary existence, heading home straight after work and writing and rewriting and plotting and not doing much else other than reading and watching movies. I haven't spent the whole last year like this, don't worry. Only the last few months because I'm so close to the end.

I've worked for so long on this novel and it's coming together at last, though I'm having problems with the ending. Maybe you'd like to read it. You always said you wanted to read it, but not until it was finished. I remember how frustrated you got whenever I started over, how you complained that I would never finish. Well, I'm almost finished. The book is set in Winnipeg now. I included some inside jokes, for Winnipeg readers. And a few for you. You always said you wanted to read it.

You don't have to read it.

So I've been reclusive but I've been getting a lot done, and feeling better about myself and my job and life in general. Your letter shocked me because it reminded me of the person I used to be. I'd almost forgotten that person but I think I may have become that person again, looking at the envelope, for a little while. But today I feel like myself and I'm looking forward to reading your letter. I've decided to open it tomorrow and read it as a birthday treat for myself. Since it arrived so close to my birthday, I assume you say "Happy Birthday" in it at some point, so that seems like the best day to read it. And if it's not a letter, but just a card, well, it's less disappointing to get a card on one's birthday.

Also, I'll need some cheering up. You know I don't like birthdays. I always feel I have to compare where I am and where I thought I'd be at that age. Well, even John Milton has written poems about this problem. ("How soon hath Time, the subtle thief of youth, / Stolen on his wing my three and twentieth year!") So maybe I make too much of things.

People will be calling all day tomorrow. I'll have to make sure the phone is plugged in. I unplug it when I'm writing. It always seems to ring when the words are flowing, and then it's like a switch has been thrown, and everything is set to off. Maybe you'll call. My number hasn't changed. If you still know my address maybe you still know my number.

~~November 2~~

~~Did you try to call~~

November 17

I still have not read your letter. I was planning to read it on my birthday. But, as predicted, I received a lot of phone calls. That was how I learned you were dead.

I received all the usual calls wishing me a happy this and good luck with that. All the usual offers to come out and have a drink. But I told everyone I just wanted to relax and read, maybe I would do something next weekend. I did not tell them *what* I wanted to read.

And I moved my laptop beside the phone in case you called and I wrote some more of my novel and almost finished it, but I am still having problems with the ending. I would say that I always have problems with endings but I have never had to deal with such an ending before, so I do not know.

In any case, I wrote and listened to some music and relaxed and planned to open your letter after dinner. I thought I would order some sushi to treat myself. And I thought about how I should get out more and decided that as soon as I had figured out this ending I would take some time off writing and do the rounds, visit my friends and go out to the bar and catch up with people. Maybe even give *you* a call, if your number hadn't changed. To thank you for your letter. I was thinking about calling you when the phone rang.

It was Gwen. She did not know that it was my birthday. She asked if I remembered her and I said of course I remembered her, she was your best friend. I said I was sorry for not recognizing her voice but it had been a long time since we last spoke.

A long time. You know how it is. Of course you know. When people break apart. How all of their friends, all of the people they know, are torn apart as well.

Gwen said she hated to tell me but somebody should tell me. She said she wasn't sure if I would have heard because we had been apart for over a year now and had no friends in common. She said that nobody was sure when it happened exactly but of course I know when it happened because I have your letter and its postmark.

I did not tell her about your letter.

She said she thought somebody should tell me because she didn't see me at the funeral and she thought I would have come. I would have come. She said she always liked me and wished things had worked out. Then she said she didn't mean it like that and of course it wasn't my fault, it wasn't anybody's fault.

She said you used pills. She said it was painless, but I do not believe her. If there was no pain, there would have been no pills.

I did not know what to say so I thanked her for calling and told her I did not know what to say.

Did you try to call? I am sorry if you tried. I had the phone unplugged. I was writing. If you called, I didn't know. I didn't ignore you.

I am not angry. I want to thank you for your letter. You did not need to send me a letter and I am glad that you did.

I promise I will read it sometime but I do not want to read it now. But I did go to my closet to search out your old letters and take them down. I read those letters and every time I finished one letter I held it while I read the next letter.

I want to thank you for writing me those three letters. You didn't have to write me any letters and it means a lot to me that you spent time writing me letters when I know you don't like to write letters. You wrote them not because you wanted to but because you knew it would make me happy to get letters from you and that means a lot to me, more than I can say.

I wonder if you kept my letters. I used to write to you all the time. I have not written to you for so long.

Every day. I will write to you every day now.

EXPLOSIONS

FIRST THERE IS an EXPLOSION, and then another EXPLOSION! The most exciting story of all time—and you're reading it.

Then you pause. All these explosions? A strong beginning, but the ending seems sure to disappoint.

But it won't! And then there is another EXPLOSION.

The explosions appear in caps, when they happen at least. Of course. EXPLOSION!

You put the story down. So far, the author has offered a good deal of excitement, but little in the way of pathos or character development. Should you keep reading?

You keep reading. And happen upon another EXPLOSION. But this one is different. This one is filled with pathos. And the character, who explodes, leads a rich inner life.

▼

YOU CAN'T JUST read about explosions all day, you're a busy executive, so you take a break and take some meetings, take some phone calls and then take up the story again, where another explosion seems poised to begin. Soon you—EXPLOSION! That one took you by surprise.

It's a rare moment when a story surprises you. As a hot-shot Hollywood producer, you read a lot of stories, and by now you can predict how most of them will develop and turn, which has flattened out your enjoyment of stories in general.

Although Hollywood long ago laid claim to excitement via explosions, this "Jonathan Ball" has put a fresh new spin on things. Should you track down the intrepid young author and purchase the film rights? You could adapt this story, "Explosions," without too much effort—of course, you would have to add a few explosions.

You ponder this, and approach the verge of a decision, but then your assistant interrupts. EXPLOSION! You hire another assistant. This next assistant you task with tracking down Ball.

"Yessir," says the assistant, eager to please. She intends to climb the ladder. Your office may be hers one day, barring unforeseen explosions.

▼

THREE WEEKS PASS, and you've forgotten about the whole thing. But then your assistant announces that Jonathan Ball is here to see you.

"Who?"

"The explosion guy."

"Oh yeah. Yeah. Send him in."

The man who enters your office looks to be in his twenties but has the greying hair of a man in his forties. His smile seems both authentic and forced, like he's happy to see you but doesn't like to smile. He wears a handsome charcoal suit, but has paired it with blue socks and white sneakers.

Ball offers his hand, a limp, pale thing, and sits without asking where. His awkward smile bleeds further across his face. And then, like he meets with Hollywood producers every day: "So what's up?"

"Well, I wanted to talk to you about your short story 'Explosions.'"

"Shoot."

"Um, okay, well, first off, I'm very interested in optioning the film rights."

"Of course."

"Yes, well, unlike most producers, I like to at least try to work with the original authors to develop the property."

Your first test, the word *property*. Most authors flinch. But Ball doesn't flinch. "Well, I've got to say, that sounds great. I always envisioned 'Explosions' as a Hollywood movie. Stylistically, it's very influenced by the work of Robert Altman and Michael Bay."

"Both Bay *and* Altman, huh?"

"Absolutely. Either of whom would be great to direct."

Altman's dead, you think, but you say, "Sure, sure. Well, I usually contract for the treatment only, because often things don't work out with the authors, but I think it's important to include them early in the process, at least. I've got more meetings lined up, but I'll have some contracts drawn up and we'll hammer this out—in the meantime, start thinking about a treatment and we'll get this ball rolling, uh, Ball."

You're often uncomfortable with writers—they're all so awkward and weird and dress like children—but Ball's presence almost makes you panic. So you whoosh him out of your office and give your new assistant a note about the contracts.

▼

IF ONLY MOVIES could be made without writers. After Ball signs the contracts, he drops by each morning to discuss the script. On the days you don't avoid him, he spends most of this time asking stupid questions. It's clear he's never written, nor even read, a screenplay before.

"So, how many times should I press the Tab key to indent the names above the dialogue?"

"You should really buy a copy of Final Draft, that screenwriting program I told you about. Or some cheaper program." Every time you see him, Ball wears the same charcoal suit. "Another writer I know swears by Highland. Actually, he invented it." You notice what looks like a mustard stain on Ball's sleeve. "Anyway, it's cheap."

"Final Draft was the name?" It's clear that Ball wants you to buy him a copy of Final Draft.

"Or Highland. Or whatever. I don't care." Is it too early to fire him? Well, yes and no. And after all, he *did* write that story. He's not incompetent, despite appearances.

You should at least see what he turns in. "In any case, you're not writing a script right now, remember? So the details of script formatting don't matter. You're only contracted to write the first draft of the treatment."

"Yes, no, *that's* underway. *That's* going well." He taps his forehead, smiles his horrible smile. "It's all up here."

"Yes, well." You stand, as you always do when someone leaves, when you want someone to leave. It takes a few moments before Ball gets the hint and scrapes away. He even has an annoying walk, his feet drag just enough to notice. But it's worse when he is standing still. He holds his feet too far apart and points his toes a bit outward, like a duck.

After Ball leaves, you move to call your assistant, but she's already in your office. She's good. Already planning to re-paint, you can see it in her darting eyes.

"I'm sorry," she says. "I say you're not in, but he just winks and walks past me."

"It's okay." Her eyes crease, she doesn't believe you. *Explosion?*

No. Not yet. "Buy him a copy of Final Draft. And tell him that the next time he comes to see me, he has to hand over the finished treatment."

She nods and you're alone.

▼

YOU MANAGE TO AVOID BALL for a few weeks by getting to the office late, making your morning calls from Starbucks. When you do see Ball next, against all expectations, he says he's got a copy of the treatment. But he won't give it to you.

"I think it's important for me to read the treatment to you, out loud, while you close your eyes and visualize it. I know that's not orthodox, but I am going to insist on this—after I do, I think you'll agree it was the best decision."

You cock your head for a second, into your hand, elbow cold against the glass of your desk. A shard of glass moves from the desk up through your arm and into your skull. Ball might drive you back to the bottle. Whatever talent he might have as a writer of explosion-laden stories pales before the awesome might of his lunacy.

But he cashed your cheque, so you might as well hear him out. If nothing else, this absurd demand will give you another reason to fire him later, if your bosses demand any reasons. Why not see it through? The worse it goes, the better.

"Sure. Make an appointment with my new assistant." The old one got too wolfish. You expect she's already a studio head somewhere else.

▼

THERE IS NO TIME that works for both you and Ball (why is he busy? what could he have to do?) except a few hours in the evening, and so you cringe as you invite Ball to your house. He arrives in a '95 red Pontiac Firefly. Dull red. Perhaps the cheapest car in all of Hollywood.

He sinks into your soft leather armchair and shuffles some papers out of a glossy black folder. Right to business, a pleasant surprise. You don't want to endure any niceties. As he slides his eyes over the pages, you tilt into the couch and wonder why it is that Ball bothers you so. Sure, he's annoying, but it's not that. There is something else, something beyond this, a buzzing whose source you can't locate.

"So, the title is the same," says Ball. "But I've made some other changes. As I'm sure you expected."

Whatever. "Why don't you just read it? We'll talk about it afterward."

"Sure." He looks at the pages for a moment, silent. He's just looking at the pages. His eyes don't move, and you get the sense that he's waiting.

Waiting for himself to begin?

Waiting for something you will do?

Then you realize. He's waiting until you see that he's waiting. And then, that you realize what he's waiting for.

This unnerves you. This isn't the bumbling Ball you thought you knew. But before you can water the thought enough for it to bloom, Ball begins to speak.

"The first explosion is a surprise. He's in a meeting, another meeting. We can see he's been in hundreds of meetings just like this. It's in his eyes, in how they stick to the empty table, and he doesn't even look up when they say he's fired.

"He just nods and they repeat it, fired. Fired yet again. This time it's the dialogue they don't like, they don't like the dialogue because it's not how people talk. It's not what people say.

"There's too much of the writer in there, too much of the writer and they aren't paying for that. They aren't paying for him to be there. They're paying for him to disappear.

"To vanish—poof!—and just leave a script behind.

"They'd like that. They'd like it if he'd just vanish. If they could put their money in a box and close the box and have there be a screenplay inside when they opened up the box again.

"Another meeting, like all the others, but something is different this time. Not in the meeting, but in its aftermath.

"They explode.

"He drives home and feeds the dogs and sighs into bed and the next morning hears the news. When they left for the day their cars exploded. They died in the explosions.

"There are theories but no explanation. He doesn't mourn and doesn't think much of it, not really.

"Not until it happens again.

"Another meeting, just like the others, but unlike the others an explosion in the aftermath. And this becomes the new routine. A meeting, an explosion. A meeting, an explosion.

"A meeting, a meeting—explosion, explosion.

"It goes on. Someone's targeting producers. Hollywood's worst nightmare. But then a change: he gets work.

"He gets work and sighs—with producers exploding all over these days, what does it matter? They'll be dead before the ink dries.

"But they aren't.

"*No explosion.*

"That's when it hits him, although it's hit the audience before this. The meetings. The firings. The explosions. There's a connection."

And Ball continues.

But you don't listen to the words anymore.

No, you listen to his voice.

To its music, its peaks and its valleys. You've located the source of that infernal buzzing.

It's right there—there, at the bottom of his voice, on the ground floor. In the way his eyes fix on the papers and don't seem to move.

When he's done, you ask not the obvious question, but the one above that. The one above, which contains the one below. "So why did you change the story?"

"I felt that things were getting too silly, too postmodern." Ball smooths his charcoal suit. Without looking, he can tell where the wrinkles are. "I wanted to bring it closer to reality."

There is nothing odd or awkward about Ball now. All the false fronts fallen away. Revealing a viper, coiled in your chair.

▼

INT. HOLLYWOOD LOSER'S OFFICE -- SOMETIME

A lavish Hollywood office. Everywhere the markers of disgusting excess: tacky awards, expensive doodads, photos of trips to exotic locales where all the locals hate you.

HOLLYWOOD LOSER smiles out of every one. A smile you just want to fucking punch.

HOLLYWOOD LOSER is a pathetic loser that feels like a big shot but is actually the fucking WORST. Just a dipshit with a bunch of stupid awards that mean nothing. Flanked by dumb tasteless bric-a-brac.

Not a speck of dust on any of this trash because they pay some halfbrain more money than I make in a year just to keep the dust off of HOLLYWOOD LOSER's shitty shit.

HOLLYWOOD LOSER sweats while eating kung pao chicken, sopping forehead swiped now and again by a fancy silk napkin that probably cost $800 for some stupid reason.

Talking on the speakerphone to SOME DICK.

                    HOLLYWOOD LOSER
               (stupidly)
          ...and so I approved his treatment.
          What else could I do? It was, uh, the
          best treatment I ever heard.

                    SOME DICK
               (angrily)
          Well, okay, but why the hell did you
          agree to pay him triple the already
          agreed-upon amount?

                    HOLLYWOOD LOSER
               (sounding extra stupid)
          Well, I wanted to pay him extra for
          the treatment and then hire someone
          else to write the screenplay. But then
          he agreed to write the screenplay for
          free, so I didn't know how to turn
          that down. I mean, what could I say?

                    SOME DICK
        What the FUCK are you talking about?!

HOLLYWOOD LOSER doesn't even know. Just a worthless
loser, remember?

Just making shit up. HOLLYWOOD LOSER has no other
option. Why pay BALL three times what they had
agreed upon?

As a bribe. As a bribe to walk away.

That was supposed to be the way out -- a payoff.
Give BALL three times what they had agreed upon,
while making it clear that the studio wouldn't
shell out the amount of money BALL was so clearly
worth for a full screenplay.

So sorry, but here's best I can do -- now walk away.

Walk away. Just walk away.

But no. He wouldn't. BALL wouldn't walk.

                    SOME DICK
        Say, "GTFO!" Say, "You're fired!" "What
        has two thumbs and fuck you? Fuck you!"

                    YOU
            (still not getting it, incredibly)
        But how? He agreed to write the
        screenplay for free!

> SOME DICK

Are you a fucking mental case? We're union. Everyone is union! He's going to have to join the union. We can't get away with paying him nothing! This is Hollywood, not your Aunt Mabel's Cookie Farm!

HOLLYWOOD LOSER does a comical head-slap -- that thing where people hit themselves in the forehead for being dumb, that stupid thing you only see in the movies.

It's all just a movie, after all.

> SOME DICK
> (getting angrier)

We can't even pay him the minimum, because the first thing that will happen is he'll get an agent, and the agent will see that you paid him three times what he was promised for the treatment, and then we are going to be totally fucked!

HOLLYWOOD LOSER squeegees brow with the expensive silk napkin or whatever the fuck it is. Sweating like a pig.

> SOME DICK
> (even more angry)

By which I mean YOU are fucked! YOU! Are! Fucked!

                    HOLLYWOOD LOSER
Let's just pull the plug. Give me the
word and I'll pull it.

Oh, really? HOLLYWOOD LOSER is going to pull the plug?

HOLLYWOOD LOSER doesn't have the guts for that.

                    HOLLYWOOD LOSER
                 (covering tracks)
I mean, if YOU pull it, I'll tell him
it's out of my hands.

                    SOME DICK
Are you kidding? You green-lit the
fucking thing! The money is being
spent, right the fuck now! The train
is on the tracks!

                    HOLLYWOOD LOSER
                 (panicked)
It's not too late. If you just say
the word --

                    SOME DICK
It IS too late, because YOU are a
fuckhead! I hope this train crashes
right into your fucking house! You're
either going to be DONE in this town,
or you are going to make me a fucking
BLOCKBUSTER and turn this train
wreck into the next...the next...

HOLLYWOOD LOSER does another comical movie-thing, rubbing temples.

They are on a speakerphone, remember, so HOLLYWOOD LOSER can rub both temples at once. Like in movies when people are supposed to look stressed out.

Just like in the fucking movies.

> SOME DICK
> ...the next whatever-the-fuck hit movie with a train in it, I don't fucking know. Was there ever a hit movie with a train? Anyway, it had better be a hit. This screenplay had better be good. Because if I end up having to fire BALL, then first I am going to fire YOU.

SOME DICK hangs up the phone or just stops talking, it's hard to tell because he's on speaker. Anyway, there is silence while HOLLYWOOD LOSER rubs temples.

Then there is a long pause, and then HOLLYWOOD LOSER clicks a button or something and that's supposed to be the phone turning off.

Then I guess we CUT or something.

"...and then you cut from the guy sitting at his desk to a later scene where the same guy is sitting at the same desk, so it's confusing visually. How does the audience know it's later, on a different day, or have any concrete idea of how much time has passed? It could be five minutes or it could be weeks, months."

You're going over the first draft of the script with Ball—the nightmare first draft, with this nightmare man.

"They'll figure it out, as the scene progresses."

You put the script down and move to rub your temples, but then catch yourself, stop. Almost pinch your nose and push fingers and thumb back to rub your eyes, but keep in control.

Instead, you place your hands palm down on the script. One on the page you're reading, one on the back of the previous page.

You breathe in, deep and slow. Breathe Ball's dead, recycled air. The two of you are too close. Crammed together in an office that never seemed so small, that felt expansive before today. Next time you should meet on the Starbucks patio or something.

Next time. Dear lord.

"But they shouldn't have to figure it out as the scene progresses. They should just know, so they can pay attention to how the scene is developing and to the story, rather than trying to figure out simple things like the fact that it's a week later."

"So what, I should add a title or something? I could put an intertitle in, like in those old silent movies, and it could say something like, *A month later, Ball has turned in his first draft of the screenplay and is getting feedback from the producer.*"

Ball should star in this film. Star as himself, like he's already doing, in this charade he presents as his life. He's the best actor you've met. A real method man.

You don't even know what to say. What do you say? The silence unfurls. Then Ball steps into the silence, to fill it with the crashing cymbals of his bullshit.

"I think that would work."

What made Ball a writer, rather than an actor, rather than a psychopathic CEO? What makes people write? There must be something horrible about writing. Something horrible that makes people horrible, like this.

"No. No, you can't...We aren't making an old silent movie, okay?"

Ball lets a grin slip—a real grin—then catches himself and turns it into a fake smile. Fake enthusiasm. "Hey, maybe we should. That would be cool."

You decide to just ignore everything, refuse to bite the hook when he casts. "The other thing is that if you were to cut from a guy sitting at a desk to him sitting at the same desk, it would be a weird jump cut, and it's visually jarring, so you need something in between to break things up."

"That's another benefit of the intertitle."

"No intertitles, just...just don't write any intertitles, okay? Figure out how to give the audience the information visually."

Ball considers this. He puts his fist under his chin, to indicate visually that he is thinking hard about amazing new and creative ideas.

You lean on your elbow, cheek in hand, close your eyes, and start rubbing your temple. Then catch yourself. Thank your stars, Ball didn't notice. In the second you closed your eyes he turned away and now stares out your office window.

Your window is really a wall, another thing that used to make this office seem large. You are seven storeys up and can see a few streets bleed down below. Ball looks out your window wall, eyes creased, a slight scowl—something out there just snagged his attention, but you can't see what.

The next thing he says pushes forward the same line of conversation but his tone is gone, he's lost his character and is just saying lines.

"How about this. The producer has the phone call, then he picks up a desk calendar. Then he turns the calendar to a month later. Then Ball walks into the office."

"Let's just talk about something else."

"Is the formatting okay?"

"Well, you don't need to keep capitalizing names. But the formatting isn't important. The problem is that you keep writing things that can't be filmed, like lengthy descriptions of a character's thoughts. While we are just looking at him onscreen. Think about the visual aspect—even though it seems like a lot is happening when you read the words on the page, the way it would translate to the audience is a guy just sitting there motionless for a long time, silent. No visual interest in the scene, and also the audience can't see what he's thinking about so they won't even understand the point of the scene."

"Well, you could film what he's thinking and show that." Ball's still looking away, transfixed by something you can't see. Just going over his lines by rote.

But it's still an improv and you still have to "yes, and" him. "If you want that, then you have to write out the stuff he's thinking about like any other visual scene. The point of the screenplay is to be a blueprint for shooting the movie. It's not a prose story. It's not about the reader. The reader isn't the audience. The reader is me, and the guy who has to go find all the props, and other people making the movie. You need to stop writing like you're writing a short story, and the audience is going to read it at some point. Nobody in the audience will ever read the screenplay. Plus, your dialogue is too long. It's too boring to watch characters talking on screen that long. That's another thing where it would be okay if someone was going to read it, but nobody except a few people plus the actors are going to read the dialogue. Just keep in mind that this is a movie, not a short story. You have to write like somebody is *watching* what you wrote. Not focus on how the words are operating like words, and telling a story with language. You aren't telling a story with language. Only your dialogue, and maybe not even that, is going to survive to make it into the movie. Those are the only words you are going to write that the audience will ever connect with. But you can't overdo it and write a ton of dialogue, and have really long dialogue sequences, it's just going to be boring and plus it will look weird onscreen with one person just sitting there and talking a lot. We aren't used to seeing that in movies so it will seem bizarre and amateur."

Ball turns back to you, his gaze hard. His character's gone and he's just the snake now. Poised to strike inside his fraying charcoal suit. "Maybe we should just fill a black screen with my words."

You don't know how to respond to this. He's not playing the game anymore. You decide to risk some snark. "That would sure make casting simpler."

Ball pulls up the left side of his mouth, in a little half-smile. He settles back into the chair, looks back out the window, relaxed now. "Well, I'll get back to work, I suppose. Although you bring up a good point. We'll have to attach a star next. Or a director?"

"Either. A star would be better."

"Let me know when we're ready to do that. I'm looking forward to meeting some stars."

You don't correct Ball. You get the message. He's going to come to the meetings. He's going to insert himself where he doesn't belong, whether you like it or not, and you'll have to cover for him, explain his presence. In other words, he's a writer-producer now. On the strength of this dipshit insult of a script.

You didn't even bother to correct the script's portrayal of Hollywood. Of course, this isn't how Hollywood works, but that's the least important thing. This isn't realism. It's the dream machine, movie magic. And all Ball has to do is act like he buys all the bullshit lies the dream factory dumped into the nation's river. You can't risk challenging him so he'll just keep rising, higher and higher, until someone gives him his own dream factory to destroy. Right after he destroys yours.

Ball rises and gathers the script from you. Even though it's your copy, not his, you turn it over. You don't want it on your desk another day.

▼

BALL SCREWS AROUND with you for a few more meetings, but then delivers a workable script. Nothing incredible, but a solid draft. The worst-case scenario. You don't have enough fuel for a fire, just for smoke.

You should have cancelled the project before now, or at least canned Ball and gotten a new writer. But neither of these are real options. Ball has eliminated your real options. And presented a serviceable script, to cut the train's brakes. You have entered Development Hell.

You don't see the benefit to Ball here. He gets paid out for the draft, but he won't get paid for more drafts unless you can move things forward in some way, and how will you move anything forward with a decent script? If it was bad, you could hire him for a new draft. If it was great, you could attach a star. But it's neither. All you can do is keep sending it around. And all everyone you send it to can do is ignore you.

You don't see what Ball is trying to accomplish, and while you plow through a bento box of mercury-laden sushi, chopsticks in one hand and cellphone in the other, watching your phone fill up with texts (the little red bubble over the big green bubble keeps flashing as the numbers change—this is your midday ritual, watching the lunchtime texts come in while you despair over what's become of your life), you realize that Ball doesn't know either.

Ball doesn't understand Hollywood. Just look at this bullshit way he depicts Hollywood in his story. He has no clue. He has no clue and he probably thinks that his script is great. Just like all those other idiot would-be screenwriters. He thinks his script is just as good as all the garbage that gets made. But he's wrong.

He may be smart, he may be a genius in his way, but he is not going to make it in Hollywood and he will never understand why. He will blame you but it is his fault. You are doing your best for him but he is the one who can't write a great screenplay. Maybe he can write a good short story but he can't write a goddamn Hollywood movie and so he's fucked and that means you're fucked. Beyond fucked. He'll kill you.

You watch the texts come in—*LOOOOOVveeeee the script!!!*—*You've done it again*—*oh man I can't get OVER how many fuckin EXPLOSIONS you worked in here*—*YES YES YES we gotta talk*—*best script I have seen for YEAAARRRSSS*—*ba-BOOM baby!!!*—one bullshit text after another. The script's fucking dead. You're dead. By the time your last chunk of fatty tuna slides down your dry throat you know your life is over. Thirty-seven texts. Thirty-seven texts and not a single phone call.

Thirty-seven lunchtime texts. Not one in the morning, not one in the afternoon. Not one all evening. The movie's dead.

▼

THEN, THE MIRACLE.

The miracle pops its own red bubble on your phone a week later. You notice it after an extra-long, extra-depressed shower. A little number 2 over the phone icon.

The first message is from Ball. That's not the miracle. "Hey, just wondering when we'll be meeting with some actors. I picked out a few scenes that would be great for auditions." Ball calling your cell, the number you never gave him. The number you never gave a single writer, ever. A belt tightens around your heart.

Then, the miracle. Christ's hand on your Lazarus script. The second message from Christopher Walken.

"Hey, you—the script. Is. Just *fascinating*. I can really, see myself. Inside! of this. And coming back, in a *big* way."

Christopher Walken. The message goes on (although at three points you think it has ended, before he starts to talk again). He loves it, impossibly. And he wants to direct. He wants to make this his directorial debut.

You can't believe your luck. Even Ball is impressed. He texts you a 😄 👐 💕 combo, which makes you want to strangle a cat.

▼

WALKEN'S LATE FOR THE MEETING, of course, but his agent arrives early. She turns out to be your old assistant, the wolfish one, who you canned under the pretence that she was stealing your nice red paperclips. Lots of regrets circling around the room now.

She gives your hand a quick, tight, painful shake. Fingernails digging. Just to let you know she didn't forget.

"Chris will be along soon." Wolfie pulls out a stick of gum, makes a show of pushing it into her mouth. Pushing it against the roof of her mouth, so that it folds. You notice this, and also that Ball's leg jitters. He's jumpy. You feel like he lost his cool to her, she somehow vampired it away.

"Would you like anything to drink?" You're talking to Wolfie but Ball answers with a request for espresso. Wolfie just shakes her head. You load up the Slayer while she continues.

"Chris loves the story. He's got some issues with the script, but nothing we can't fix. He's been looking for a project like this for a while. Something hip and weird and fun and thrilling, a real thriller, with some mystery in there. And something substantial to say, you know. About the creative process. Anyway, he can tell you all about it."

You nod—just meaningless chatter to kill time, why bother even opening your mouth?—but Ball seizes on something she said. "Issues with the script?"

"There's always issues." You eye-dagger Ball. "We're still in development." Fuck you, Ball. Fuck you. Don't blow this. There is one—ONE, *lit-er-al-ly* ONE—person on this planet who gives even the *tiniest* fuck about your script. And that person is Christopher Walken. So shut up.

Ball's about to reply but then Walken and your assistant burst through the door, Walken somehow both leading and being led by the assistant. He sees Wolfie and claps, smiles. Opens his arms up, fingers spread, the way he does.

"Let's get TO it, I—have got to *tell* you, never...have I been so. Excited—by a, script!"

Ball's starstruck. "Wow, I mean, thanks, I mean—"

You shove an espresso into his face just to stop from killing him.

Walken's found a chair and somehow edged himself into one quarter of it. "I've been, waiting, to di-*rect* something but it NEEDED to be. Special and—to have a soul. Plus a lot of explosive *stuff* and you know. This, just. Fits."

Ball opens his mouth so you rush words out of yours. "And you're thinking of starring as well?"

"Well. I love to play, a—writer! They always have a lot of...Do I, smell. Espresso?"

You almost jump. "Yes, let me get you one. Sorry."

Wolfie smiles, she's enjoying this. Well, good, somebody should. She takes over as you operate the devilish contraption. "Chris just thinks we need some shifts. The revelation that the writer is behind everything after all seems weak. I mean, who would believe that a *writer* would have any guts? Writers are passive and weak and victims of a system, everyone knows that. Instead, maybe the writer has a dark twin, like a shadow figure or something, like a *Dark Half* sort of thing."

"The Stephen King movie?" You're trying to remember.

"It was a book," says Ball.

No shit, Ball. Every movie was a book. "Ah yes. The one about the writer. With a supernatural twin, sort of haunting him, but sort of alive in a way too. Like, a ghost writer."

"You see, what I mean. It *seems* like he's. Doing it all. But then we find the—...truth."

"A parasitic twin, that got absorbed but then comes back like a guardian angel and kills the producers until he gets the job, and then starts helping him write, like taking over and making him write things he doesn't want to write. And then his family begins to feel threatened too." Wolfie's sparking. You can see where all this is headed and you don't know how to stop it. You don't know if you should.

"But that's not the story." Ball's out of the shallows now. About to drown. "He doesn't have a family, he doesn't have a twin. There's nothing supernatural going on."

"And. He ends up in a room, where. They finally face—as his *wife* worries, which one. Is he really?"

You hand Walken his espresso—and you have to admit, after all these years in this horrible town, you still get a bit of a jolt handing Christopher Walken an espresso. "The Romero film came out in 1993. Do you know where the rights stand?"

"MGM absorbed Orion. I don't think there's a project."

"I'll call. We'll work things out."

And then it's over. The meeting's done. The fish hauled into the boat—it flops around some, but it's dead. It just doesn't know.

Ball doesn't know. But you can see it. You can see the knowledge coming. As he sips his espresso. And his eyes go glassy as the life drains out.

All your worrying, and yet the answer was before you all along. How does one combat a writer's insanity? With an actor's insanity, of course.

Walken swallows the rest of his espresso in one gulp and rises with another clap. You want to clap too. Quite the performance. The movie based on Ball's short story just became a remake of *The Dark Half*. Starring Christopher Walken in his directorial debut. A Hollywood meeting at its finest.

Instead of killing you, Ball killed himself. You court the Beast and get a horn up your ass.

As Walken's leaving, Ball calls him back. "What was it. The thing writers always have. Why you wanted to play one." He's so broken he can't even inflect his questions.

Walken scowls, then plasters back his smile. "They always have a, lot. Of *depth*."

Ball nods, as rocks tumble down his abyss.

▼

THE TRACKS LAID, you sit back and watch the movie move forward. Wanting always to reach out for the brake. But the train speeds ahead, coward that you are. You secure the rights. The budget climbs.

Ball executes a nightmare second draft. Incorporates only the barest elements of the original King story. Doesn't change the title. But you can confront him now. The situation has changed, now that Walken pilots the project.

"I don't see why I have to make all of these changes. He loved the original script."

"Yes, well, irregardless." You know that *irregardless* is a word that really pisses off writers.

"Maybe we should find another star."

"There isn't another star. There's only Walken. And this is how it works with stars."

"What about my copyright?"

"You don't have copyright. This isn't books. You sold your rights to the studio, and we packaged them together with the rights to *The Dark Half,* and now they belong to Christopher Walken. Technically, you don't even work for me anymore."

"I don't work for anyone."

"Well, on paper you work for Walken now and I buffer him from you. And I work for this studio, which has a financial stake in Christopher Walken's directorial debut, but has ceded final cut to Walken himself. So in a way, I work for him too."

"How did Walken get final cut?"

"He's Christopher Walken. And this is his directorial debut. Plus PR stuff. It increases the Oscar buzz."

Just shut up, Ball. Shut up and hang up and write your drivel and maybe you'll win a fucking Oscar. Your head hurts and this time you really do have Ball on speakerphone so you give in and rub your temples.

▼

THE MOVIE SLUDGES FORWARD. Ball turns in another draft, a passable one, and Walken sends it back without anyone having read it. Just the vague instructions that it needs to be "punched up." You aren't going to waste time with a punch-up meeting so you just make up some gibberish demands to keep Ball busy.

He does another draft filled with philosophical asides, and you simply cross them all out and send it back without even forwarding it on to Walken.

Then Ball does another draft, a surprise improvement. Maybe as his spirit breaks, he will learn to survive Hollywood. Walken sends it back with all the dialogue punctuation in different places.

Next, Walken demands a further change, which you have to relay to Ball. The final major change, the inevitable change.

The words you have been waiting for, handwritten on Walken's personal stationery. Five words, five beautiful words. All alone, clustered halfway down the page, a whole letter in five words.

Take out all the explosions.

▼

THE TRAIN SPEEDS toward its tunnel, as movie trains do. Will it glide through the tunnel, or scrape off its sides? Will those battling atop the train duck or get decapitated? Is the tunnel real, or painted on stone? Until the movie train hits the tunnel, no one will know.

It takes Ball a long time to submit his final draft. But he does. He submits through the mail—through the fucking *paper mail*—packaged inside the box that once held his fraying charcoal suit.

Just when you think you've seen it all. Ball's a travesty. But the script's perfect. Not a single explosion mars its flawlessly formatted pages.

▼

YOU DON'T SEE BALL AGAIN. He doesn't show to the meetings you call him to, gives no excuses. So you make excuses for him, lie like it's your job. Lucky for you, it *is* your job.

He doesn't answer email. He doesn't pick up his phone. The one time you manage to get through, Ball pretends to be his own personal assistant, assures you he will relay your message.

The movie train speeds. For an instant, it seems like it might run off its rails. Someone calls the set, issues a bomb threat. If production continues, there will be explosions.

The set shuts down. But Walken's representatives spin it for publicity. A movie about explosions delayed due to the threat of explosions! (They neglect to mention that all the explosions were taken out, instead playing up its one-time basis in Ball's story.) It's a marketing wet dream. Things go over budget, but then because of the publicity they just raise the budget. There's not another bomb threat.

By the time of the premiere, you have all but forgotten Ball. In the end, the movie works. Walken glows, the writer's madness radiating from his sallow moon of a face. Even the more awkward lines of dialogue sound brisk when delivered the Walken way.

Then the near-forgotten Ball appears next to you, in a seat reserved for your plus-one. Who couldn't make it (because *You can go fuck yourself!*) and didn't mention this in time for you to give away the ticket.

Ball's charcoal suit looks like he's been sleeping in it and seems bulked-up, like he's let himself go. Although he's clean-shaven and his shoes are polished. The sharpness returned to his eyes and he unnerves you again.

Careful, holding steady in a small-talk tone, you risk a question. Just to get some reaction, to judge Ball's new mood. "Tell me something. I always wondered—why did you choose to write the story in the second person?"

Ball looks up, but not at you. At the black void of the unlit screen, as if the answer lies there. No, as if the screen were an enemy, triumphant, the victor in some contest of wills, and Ball a bitter, defeated supplicant.

Or maybe the opposite. When he speaks, his voice is steady. He seems controlled. And he's not playing anymore. He's telling you the truth, and this scares you. You're about to watch a so-called thriller, but you know what it really is. All of Walken's slick direction can't hide its origins, can't erase its core.

It's a horror film. A classed-up horror film. And in horror, in true horror, the monster never loses. The monster never dies. The monster is the truth.

Ball doesn't look at you, just keeps staring at the screen. Smiling an impossible smile. "I wanted to write the story in the second person because all of the stories in the second person are so lousy. I wanted to do things the wrong way, the way I was always told not to do them, just to prove I could. Take the error toward perfection, into impossible realms.

"But I couldn't make it perfect. I couldn't make it perfect and I couldn't make them cry where I cry. They don't move to its rhythm in the manner I imagined. They don't understand the terror of a sentence that took me weeks.

"They don't feel its blade. A bone knife edged in diamond. Drawn out from its birthplace inside me, through a wound that will never heal. The story merciless, triumphant. Flaunting my failure to exceed it. It grins death in the face of my dumb hope, that I might find words adequate to its end."

You notice now, for the first time, that Ball holds something. He clutches it like a child clutches fingers while crossing the street. But you can't see what it is. You can't see what he holds, clasped tight in his palm, held close to his chest, against his bulky, unravelling suit.

Outside the theatre, something explodes in the distance. Then something else. Tinny, wilted sounds.

But getting louder. Moving closer.

"Words adequate to its end." Ball echoes himself and stares up at the screen. Clasps something tight. Face split, like the viper's it is, in a vicious, eternal smile.

NOT WHAT SHE EXPECTED, these stories. Aleya can't discern any message. She thought it would somehow be obvious. As different as these stories are, they seem like a suite of sorts, Ball moving through the phases of a career, through different skins. But who is this writer of hers? The more his name appears, the less defined he seems to be.

She looks up at the wall, where she has hung an empty frame. She likes to look at the frame and at the wallpaper inside it—the wallpaper that, unframed, she would ignore. The empty frame is her reminder to herself that she must pull herself into the present, into noticing. Her private meditation. It hangs in front of the couch right where another house might hold a television. She tries to look at it, to pay attention, whenever she feels herself drifting.

There is always a part of me that is detached and observing. I might have made a good writer. But growing up in the bookstore inoculated her against writing. So few came in, so few bought what they browsed. Some of the books never moved from the time they were put on the shelves to the day her mother remaindered them. Father being too sensitive to tear off their covers.

Aleya stares at the yellow wallpaper, yellowing further inside its frame. One of those sprawling, flamboyant patterns. And for the first time realizes she doesn't like it, never liked it. Hates it. She only loves the frame.

▼

WHAT IS HE TRYING TO TELL HER? Her throat dry, but her coffee gone. Aleya hasn't noticed herself drinking it. She sets the book down, takes the cup to the sink. Fills it, gulps the water, gasps.

She turns to place her back against the kitchen counter and regard the couch. The book lies there, spread face down to keep her place, the way her father had always complained about, saying it broke the spine. *How would you like a broken spine?* he asked her once. He was being playful, but it sounded so violent that even much later it outwrestles many other memories of him, comes into her head unbidden, forcing out better moments from the pleasant childhood he worked so hard to craft for her.

Her throat still dry, so she fills the cup again. As she often does as the evening wears on, she realizes that hours have passed without her speaking. She's been silent since she left the tea house. Another memory rises in her, of a time she had been playing in the bookstore while a writer spoke to her parents. No, just to Father, when Mother was upstairs rearranging the shelves, a job Aleya was supposed to have helped her with. But Aleya had gone downstairs to use the bathroom and detoured to scour the magazine racks. The writer, a regular, apologized to her father for a raspy voice. The woman had been under a crushing book deadline, and was at home working straight through this day and the last, and so she hadn't spoken aloud since two nights earlier, when she'd had dinner with friends. Some people spoke to themselves, the writer supposed, but she did all of that sort of talking on the page.

Aleya never forgot that conversation and often remembers it on these nights when her throat goes dry. She is rarely lonely, enjoys her solitude, but at such times wonders about its wisdom. She decides to speak aloud. But what will she say? What to say to the air, to the cold evening, to the onrushing night?

Then the kettle whistles, startling her.

Aleya rushes to take it off the stove. She doesn't remember starting the kettle. She remembers making coffee in her French press and running the kettle then, but that was back before she started the book. Now the coffee was gone. She came to the kitchen for water and drank the water, but had she started the kettle?

She must have. The kettle just whistled, so she had to have started the kettle.

But she doesn't want more coffee. And she doesn't remember it. Of course, this is not truly that strange. We don't notice ourselves doing many things. She is just unnerved by the sudden sound. She read a book a few weeks back about neuroscience, which posited that most of our actions are unconscious motions initiated by our bodies. We are a collection of routines and subroutines, zombie-like automatons, and our consciousness just kicks in now and again with veto power to cancel actions. These conscious decisions, though they constitute little of our lives, ingrain new routines and subroutines. (*Habits*, why not just say *habits*? Like many popular science books, the writing is atrocious.) Anyway, the upshot of it all, as she understands things, is that you don't remember doing most things because what you think of as *You* doesn't do them. You just let your body, or what the book describes as "your zombie," do them without interruption. She watched a documentary once where the philosopher Slavoj Žižek talked about the movie *Alien* and offered a similar idea while comparing Freud's thought with the horror movie trope of possession or parasitism: "We are the aliens controlling our animal bodies."

Aleya likes that. Makes her think of when you read a novel and your mind starts filling in the details. The writer says the woman goes to the kitchen to get some water and you see that her cup is black with pink trim. That her couch is plush blue microfibre. You know she started the kettle because you are told that it whistles, even if the writer never told you she started it, even if she doesn't remember herself.

You watch her mind drift before she notices it drifting. But then she notices and she puts her cup down, into the sink. Too sad to rinse it like she usually would. Disappointed.

She thought she would feel relief to see the dedication appear like an afterthought, or a lark, rather than something from which the whole project proceeds. If her writer just made a poor decision after writing the book, rather than planning the whole book for her. But Aleya does not want to be an afterthought. She wants to be part of his plan.

She takes her cup back out of the sink. The kettle had boiled, so she must have turned it on, she must have wanted coffee, so she makes some more coffee. This way it will all make sense, after the fact. She will have done things for a reason, set the water to boil with clear purpose. When the coffee is ready Aleya sips it standing up, back against the smooth concrete counter. The cold of the counter and the warmth of the coffee filling her stomach meet and clash at the small of her back.

What a cool night it is becoming, for summer. She wonders if it might rain.

▼

SOMEHOW, ALEYA FINDS HERSELF on the couch with her coffee, with the book. She decides to think through the stories so far. But she doesn't know what to think, and it's cold. She sets her coffee down (you imagine a table that she sets the coffee upon) and moves to the thermostat. Cranks it up and sits down on the heat register, pulling her shirt and sweater out and hooking them around the register grille to capture the air. She used to do this as a child, and her parents always yelled at her, but now this is *her* house. The furnace kicks in with a metallic grunt, and warm air gusts up and over to stroke the skin of her back.

But she can't get warm. She wonders if the book is what chilled her, but she doesn't know why that should be.

She is afraid to start the book again. She has started to want a message. Wants him to speak to her. She does not want to want this.

To Aleya, who will learn why.

An impossible promise. A promise to speak to her, but a book only speaks to its reader, to an abstraction that does not exist. Even now that Aleya *is* the reader, the connection is imaginary, fake. She rises and goes to the window. Her living room overlooks an empty street and a parking lot, a waste of a picture window. The light in the lot has burnt out. Night empty and growing more cold.

She feels trapped in her house, behind her window's glass. Outside, in the darkened lot, in the empty street, the world goes on. Inside, she feels frozen beside the book. She will escape. She takes the book out to the porch, to read the rest in its dull mothlight.

But not a single insect flutters there. This disturbs her. The night far too quiet.

She steps down from the porch, crosses over the sidewalk and into the street. Her road is never busy at night, but never this quiet. She doesn't even hear crickets.

She listens for traffic, but hears nothing. She considers walking out toward the Sunnyside LRT station. She can see its glow in the distance. The tea shop lies beyond that, windows dark.

Aleya stands in the street and looks up into the sky. Thinks about walking down the dark road through the silence, beneath the stars. People always say you can't see the stars in a city, but she has always been able to see the stars. Maybe that doesn't apply to Canada or maybe she has always been lucky.

As a child she slept on the porch in the summertime, something she still can't believe her parents allowed. A kid in the country maybe, but in the city? Other nights, in her teens, she snuck out of her bedroom window onto the roof and lay counting stars, marvelling at their distance.

She used to reach up her hand, as if to touch them, then yank it back and pretend she had been burnt.

What she loves about the stars is their distance, and the uncaring way that they burn. How they are burned away by now. She loves feeling unimportant to them, unimportant to the planet. She loves the cold of the indifferent night.

Maybe she is just a downer, and it isn't the book's fault. She likes her melancholy. She likes being alone with it. Is this so wrong? She likes her books because they let her be alone.

COSTA RICAN GREEN

THE SUN THAT SHINES on the Caribbean Sea is a brighter sun than the one that shines on Winnipeg. There must be two suns. There must be a sun that shines between songs, or when your lover laughs, or when you are in Panama with one of your best friends, your friend from across the ocean that you never get to see. It must be a different sun than the one that burns your skin and fades your pictures and blinds you while you drive to work.

And if there are two suns then it stands to reason there are two worlds. There must be a world we see and a world that stays hidden. And which sun shines down upon which world, and whether we are shadows or flesh or somehow something of both, are mysteries. And will remain mysteries.

▼

WHILE WAITING FOR VIRPI TO ARRIVE, I walk and write and film the city. The sun wafts down over streets filled with broken things: bottles, toys, pavement, tree branches. The streets are all numbered in San José, Costa Rica, and after a few mistakes I come to understand the numbering system. Now it's impossible to become lost. I am alone for a few days before Virpi arrives and I spend them exploring, in the limited way that one can explore, alone, in the wrong language.

My Spanish consists of *I don't understand Spanish* but many people speak English, a broken English that drops out onto the street. I haven't travelled much, never to any place where English isn't the first language, so even the simplest interactions are glazed exotic. It is strange for my language to fail me, and I withdraw, wounded, from most conversations.

I spend most of my time alone, before Virpi arrives. I collect things: new words from billboards and graffiti, new food from the many restaurants, new warmth from the calm bright sun, new sights with my camera and pen. I write a journal where I record a few impressions and some of my more memorable jaunts. When I stop to write—on a patio outside a cracked yellow café with pink awnings, on a stone bench in a small park beside a domed platform and scores of cooing pigeons, standing up in a fruit market with Spanish ringing through the streets—people watch me, and their watching makes my writing feel important. I think of Hemingway, wonder if this is why he wrote in cafés in Paris, but then remember it had more to do with the noise from the sawmill below his apartment.

This city is quiet, quieter than any city I have ever been in, and it is easy to sit and write outside, something I could never do in Canada.

▼

I PHOTOGRAPH EVERYTHING. I have a cheap camera I bought for the trip, an automatic I don't mind losing or having stolen. I heard and read that theft was a problem in Costa Rica, but see no evidence of this while travelling, and often wish I had brought my expensive still camera. The other camera I have with me is a Super 8 movie camera, an old model I bought for six dollars at a Salvation Army store. I learned how to process certain black-and-white motion picture film stocks in five-gallon pails at the Winnipeg Film Group, so I film everything, wanting raw footage I can develop and manipulate by hand.

Everywhere I go, I scavenge for images. A house sagging inside a steel cage. Rings of barbed wire, looped over endless brittle walls. Pavement shattered, spreading out, as if hammered by the fist of a god. Fruit and vegetables rolling and rotting in the market streets. The jagged skyline, houses fluttering up and down the hilly terrain. Birds strutting down the streets, wheeling through the air.

Birds and water are what I photograph the most. Birds and water and stone. Their patterns. All of these images I plan to alter. I can change their colours, tint them, tone them, obliterate parts of them, erase them from the world or the world from around them, redirect their motions, intercut or juxtapose them with each other. I can do almost anything with my hands, anything else with computers.

The patterns are what I am after. Not the birds or the water or the stones, or the way the trees move, or the look on a face noticing me for the first time, but the patterns of these things: how the birds circle, how the water flows, where the streets are worn, how the mouth is beginning to open before the shot ends, before it speaks.

▼

VIRPI'S HOME IS HELSINKI, FINLAND. She has been travelling around South America, in Brazil mostly, for about a month before she steps off the plane in Costa Rica. I'm only taking a short trip, meeting her here, and it's the farthest from home I have ever been. We plan to travel together for a few days before returning to our own countries. We had planned to spend some time together in New York, a short visit for me and a stopover for her on the final leg of her South American trip, but I learned that it was cheaper to go to Costa Rica for ten days than it was to go to New York City for four.

When Virpi steps off the plane I think she is a ghost, so perfect a picture she strikes, so precisely like my memories. I can't believe in her at first. It has been seven years since I last saw her. I know she must have changed. But here she is—hair dyed the same deep black, cut long and falling in sharp contrast against the same pale skin. Even after a month of travelling through South America, under the blazing summer sun, her skin is the same pale white. When she spots me with the same quick eyes she smiles the same broad smile. I wish I had my camera.

After that lost moment I am never without my camera.

▼

WE DECIDE TO GO TO PANAMA, to a group of small islands in the Caribbean. We'll take a bus from San José to Sixaola and cross the border there. Once in Panama, we'll take a cab along some back roads to the sea, then a water taxi across the Caribbean to our chosen hotel. We try to call the hotel, a small resort on Isla Colón near Bocas del Toro, and make reservations. After a short telephone call to the woman at the hotel, who responds to my request for reservations with "Oh, you don't need reservations," we decide it's safe to assume we'll find a room on the islands somewhere, if not there. We plan our route and decide that if we leave early in the morning we can be on Isla Colón before midnight.

This is assuming anything is on or near schedule. Schedules mean very little here. Virpi has been travelling for some time and has great tales of transportation mishaps.

"While taking a train in Brazil," she says in her careful, measured purr, "I was delayed for almost a full day after we hit a man on the tracks."

"What was he doing?"

"He was just lying there, in the middle of nowhere."

"Did he want to get hit?"

She shrugs. "You look very different."

"You look exactly the same."

"I am very different."

▼

MY GUIDEBOOK DESCRIBES SIXAOLA as "a dirty, unattractive town with nothing to offer except for a relatively lax border crossing into Panama," but fails to add, "which closes very early each day." After a long bus ride past many banana trees, their brilliant green and yellow stripping down to my black and white, we disembark beside a convenience store and stumble into a tall, skinny Jamaican who appears before us to proclaim us that the border is closed. We'll have to stay in Sixaola overnight. He'll agree to be our guide for a tip.

The man talks fast and thick. His smile is at once friendly and disparaging. He's annoying, but seems harmless. "There are two hotels. Do you want the nice hotel or the cheap one?"

"What's the difference?"

"One has hot water."

I've learned that "hot water" often means a device attached to the shower head that will electrocute you while it warms the water. "The cheap one is fine, as long as it's nearby."

"Everything is near in Sixaola!" He starts to march away down a street-long puddle of mud, waving for us to follow.

▼

THE HOTEL CONSISTS of two rooms above a loud, rancid bar. Our room is just larger than the mattress, and the doors close with padlocks. The bartender gives us a key for our padlock and we decide to go back to the convenience store and look for something to eat rather than risk the bar food. We give our guide a smaller tip than he seems to expect and he grumbles away but promises to come back in the morning and get us a cab across the border. We can't find anything appealing in the store so we end up dining on a loaf of plain white bread.

We are sharing a mattress so we sleep in our clothes. The occupants of the other room keep us up all night with their screaming—after about three minutes of sex-screaming, they settle into an hour of fight-screaming, repeating this cycle. When they finally fall asleep, the dogs on the street outside pick up the slack. We find this all very funny and stay up most of the night, chatting. When we finally doze off, we dream of leaving Sixaola.

▼

THE NEXT DAY OUR "GUIDE" leads us through the border, which is crossed by walking over a rickety bridge above a small stream a long way down. The bridge is only open to foot traffic due to its weakness and its many holes. I am afraid of heights, and trail far behind Virpi, testing each step. Panama Customs doesn't seem to care who we are as long as we pay the "entrance fee," which seems suspiciously like a regulated bribe. Our guide lives up to his promise and has a cab waiting for us when we leave the office.

The cabbie is a pleasant change from our sullen but smiling guide. Virpi and the cabbie chat in Spanish while I listen and try to pick up words. He teaches me a few phrases I forget almost instantly and, with Virpi's help, I translate some things into English for him and coach his pronunciation, common phrases he wants to know for when he deals with American tourists. We reach our water-taxi stand, tip him well, and arrange for him to pick us up on the way back in a few days.

After our brief stay in the mud pit of Sixaola, it's nice to be back in the country, amongst the greenery again, miles and miles of bananas and plantains (our cabbie stops and buys us plantains after I confess that I've never eaten one). It begins to rain just before we ride out in the water taxi, a refreshing rain. I take some pictures of Virpi and run my movie camera while we travel on the water, filming animals and birds and the ripples of the rain.

▼

WE END UP GETTING OUR ROOM on Isla Colón after all, a small shack all to ourselves, rising out of the sea on stilts. We have more beds than we need this time, and a back door that opens onto the sea. We dangle our feet in the warm water and pull them out when we see a small ray, afraid it might sting us. Geckos are everywhere. When I shower I see a gecko in the shower with me, and when I dress I find a gecko in my sock. Body and head, they are about as long as my middle finger, tail trailing away another pinkie. They change colour, which I wasn't aware geckos could do. They are so many things I do not know.

Our resort is a collection of five similar shacks and a large patio that serves as a lobby and breakfast nook. The owner also keeps snorkelling gear in the backroom for customers to borrow. The resort is isolated from the rest of the island, so it hosts a large dock where water taxis arrive and depart a few times a day or whenever they are called. Bocas del Toro is just a short ride away, a small tourist town with a handful of stores and restaurants.

It's the rainy season, which means it rains almost every day, if only a little, and is cooler than normal. When I was still at the hostel in San José and could check my email, I learned that it was the same temperature in Costa Rica as in Winnipeg, only a little more humid. Panama is colder—still warm, but colder than Winnipeg at the moment. We explore the town and the beach. It's a bit too cool to swim today so we spend most of our time talking and relaxing, wandering around, taking pictures.

▼

FOR SOMEONE WHO has never travelled farther than a few states into the US, it's strange to be so far away from home yet for some things to be so familiar. Before Virpi arrives, I photograph a wall in San José that reads *Bush Asesino*, a phrase I see repeated in graffiti everywhere I go and that must mean either *Bush Is an Assassin* or *Assassinate Bush*. Travelling with Virpi, I learn that the official currency of Panama is the US dollar. The economy of Costa Rica is, I'm told, dependent on US tourism, and everywhere I go I am mistaken for an American. I tell people that I am Canadian, but they don't understand the difference.

I'm not sure I understand the difference. In Panama and Costa Rica, the streets are lined with booths that sell the same junk jewellery that people sell in Winnipeg, at festivals and in the malls. The one interesting booth I see is run by a man selling handcrafted pan flutes. I pay for one and he makes it in front of me. The man plays me a short tune before he hands it over, but to this day I cannot get it to make any sound.

In Bocas del Toro I buy some beach sandals, which fall apart in two days. Virpi sees a sign and squeals. The sign advertises day trips to swim with dolphins.

"That sounds like fun, but look at the dates. The tours don't start up again for a few weeks."

"Not that. Look here."

I follow Virpi's finger to the bottom of the sign, where large asterisks enclose the words *Dolphins Included in Price.*

"It's a good deal for dolphins," she giggles.

"Yes, but I don't think they'll let you take them through customs."

"Now, that is worth taking a picture of. Better than your rocks and barbed wire." She strolls away, laughing.

▼

I TAKE MY CAMERA EVERYWHERE, film everything. Virpi shakes her head. "You're going to fall in a hole."

"After I develop the film, I'm going to do some hand manipulation—scratch up the images, dye them different colours, maybe paint on them."

"I am going to carve a word into the sand."

"I even have some found footage of Mexico that was lying around the film group, junk footage for workshops. I'm going to make a movie mixing this film with these home videos from Mexico somebody took in the seventies or eighties. No one will even notice."

"There. I will draw a big heart around the word too."

"I am committed to deceiving my audience. It's part of a poetics of corruption I'm working on."

"You should call the film *Costa Rican Green* but then dye it red and fill it with pictures of Mexico."

"I can't read your writing. What does it say?"

"It's a Finnish word: *tenttikirja.* It means 'textbook' but everyone will think it is the name of somebody's lover."

▼

WE HAVE A LOT TO TALK ABOUT. We haven't seen each other for a long time, and have kept in touch, but in spurts. And the mundane activities of the days and weeks tend not to get mentioned, only the large events, when really it is these mundane activities that constitute our lives. And so there is something missing in letters and on the phone, even though we remain close and comfortable with one another.

"It is good to see you. It's been so long."

"It's good to see you too."

"The wind is picking up."

"Did you sleep well?"

"The wind is salty, so strange."

"Here, let me show you some pictures."

"Amazing."

"I want to stop and write out some postcards."

"Maybe I can send that letter."

"This is my dog—but you've seen my dog in pictures already."

"It would be nice to swim tomorrow, if it's warmer."

"Have you ever gone snorkelling?"

"I wonder how the water tastes, if it tastes like the wind."

"Look at that. Those houses. They've fallen into the sea. All that stone. Just broken off like that, one wall standing, the rest below. Come here, look. Do you see? I wonder how it happened. Solid stone, must be cement. See down there, in the water, parts of the floor and the roof, sticking out. There must be five houses. Maybe there were more before. I wonder when it happened. Look out those windows. All those grey walls, then the road and the trees beyond it. Or if you look the other way, into the house, there's no glass in the window, and nothing inside, just the sky and the sea where there should be a wall. No doors. All the doors must have faced the sea. Think of all those doors now, buried in the sea bed. I wonder if they are opened or closed. Do you think that anybody was hurt? Where did they go, after? I don't see any other houses around here. We're too far from the town, just the beaches and the cemetery and these houses. Put that camera down. I wonder about those doors."

▼

WHEN VIRPI DRAGS ME away from my camera we go snorkelling.

Virpi wants to see some fish. It doesn't look like there are many fish, but it's the warmest day yet, and snorkelling is a good way to cool off. The water is clear and you can see all the way to the bottom in most parts. A few small fish flit here and there. I let myself sink into the water, the seaweed rising around me, and in an instant there are thousands of fish, more sizes and shapes and colours than I ever dreamed there could be. It seems like another world, one that vanishes as soon as I lift my head above the water.

▼

DID ANY OF THIS ACTUALLY HAPPEN? I only know what I filmed, without sound.

I do not even know that.

Travelling in Costa Rica and Panama is not the journey I want to write about. The important journey is hidden. There are worlds beneath words, between lines.

▼

FOR EVERY SECOND YOU WATCH A FILM, you see twenty-four separate photographs with tiny flashes of darkness between each picture, timed so your eye doesn't notice the shift from one photograph to the next and they don't blur together. Motion is an illusion created by viewing these photographs rapidly, in sequence. Movement is precisely what is missing from a movie. The blank space between two frames of film, what occurs during that fraction of a second, what cannot be imprisoned by the camera. What we believe we are seeing.

When I watch the film in my apartment in Winnipeg, what strikes me most is a rather uneventful half a minute during the short water-taxi trip back to the mainland, beginning the journey home. I film the sun glinting off the water on my side of the boat, then turn the camera on Virpi. She spies me, flashes a sunny smile, waves at the machine.

Watching the film in my apartment, I notice for the first time that, for a split second before she saw the camera, before she flashed that smile, Virpi wore the saddest expression I have ever seen on another person.

I run the film backwards, and there she is—smiling, waving, lowering her hand, her smile, her eyes. I take the film out of the projector and look at it under a magnifying glass. Just before that smile, that sudden burst of light, for less than a second, on a few frames of film, is a woman I do not know, I did not see, even when I was looking straight at her. Then, somewhere between two of the tiny photographs, during a fraction of a second, this woman I do not know vanished and the Virpi I know took her place.

What happened then, in that moment? In a world forever lost to me, one that lived and died in an instant? I want to find that woman, ask her name. Tell her that I love her. That whatever it was, I am sorry for not seeing it.

▼

THE MORE I LOOK UPON THIS WORLD, the more I realize I do not know this world.

I do not know the sun, the sea, or even my own shadow.

JUDITH

SCOTT REFUSED THE MACHINES. But then Judith.

Who wanted to go skydiving. Who found a company that would drop them over Hawai'i Volcanoes National Park, where they could see the ocean, volcanoes, and lava fields on the way down, and then land just beyond this glorious but hazardous scenery.

A beautiful, once-in-a-lifetime thing. The perfect way to begin a honeymoon.

Scott balked. What if something went wrong? A shame to survive the wedding only to die on the honeymoon.

She didn't laugh. So they fought.

Too risky, too worrying. She wasn't worried. They'd book it now, he'd have a year to worry about it, but then they *were* jumping out of the plane.

And if something happened? Nothing would happen. But if he was so worried, he could ask the machines.

He stalled. "What machines?"

"You know." She lit a cigarette. She was quitting as a wedding gift but not for another month.

The death machines. They drew some blood, analyzed it somehow, and spit out a piece of paper explaining how you would die. No one knew how the machines worked, even their manufacturer. But they worked. They were never wrong, though frustrating, vague.

"It'll ease your mind," she said, "when it doesn't say *sky-diving* or something like that. You'll see there's no reason not to go."

He said the machines were dangerous. That they worked by suggestion, crafting random but self-fulfilling prophecies. She scowled and told him that was crap, a conspiracy theory. Besides, it didn't change things. They were never wrong, and whatever fate the machine outputted, be it *gunshot* or *choking* or *tsunami* or *sex with pit bull*, it wouldn't be *skydiving* and that was that.

And if it was, well, then she'd give up and they wouldn't go. Although it would still happen sometime, somehow, because the machines were never wrong.

But he didn't want to know.

"That's nonsense. You're just afraid. Everyone wants to know. It's freeing." Judith had gone years ago, when the machines were first released for public use. *Bus*, the machine said, and since then she'd cultivated a taste for things like skydiving. And though she didn't believe you could escape your fate, she avoided public transit.

She was right. He was afraid. But he denied it, so they fought some more.

In the end, though, he gave in. The perfect wedding gift. And though he couldn't admit it, she was right. He wanted to know.

▼

THE MACHINES WERE IN ALL THE MALLS, so Judith took him shopping. She let him pick out something from a lingerie shop, as a *thank you* for agreeing to go. "Don't think too much about it." She waved the small bag in front of his face. "Think about this instead."

He asked what it was like, when she went. She twisted her purse strap. "I'll be honest, at first it's terrible. A real shock. You want to know more, but the machine won't tell you more. If you do it again, anytime, at any machine, it's always the same prediction. After a few days, though, it feels great. You feel helpless, so you don't have to worry. I don't even notice the buses anymore."

He was distracted and anxious all day, so she told him jokes and smiled her best smiles. He thought about the lingerie, tight against her tanned thighs, and how happy she'd be in the air, lava fields beneath them.

They shopped and ate some pizza, closing a narrowing spiral around the mall's death machine, putting it off. He felt sick and the pizza made him feel sicker and he decided to stop putting it off.

The machine looked like an instant-photo booth, black and orange like some child's toy but marked with the grey image of an ancient stone face. A Greek mask of Apollo, painted on the side.

Apollo's face severe, his mouth a gaping O.

Thick dark cloth hung over the booth's entrance. Scott parted the black and stepped inside.

He hadn't told Judith, but it was his second time inside this booth. When the machine was first installed he came to it, alone. Before they met. He waited for a long time— the line stretched halfway down the mall that day, as they did everywhere when the machines were new—and when his turn came, he sat inside, looked at his hands, and went home.

Now he looked up into the mask of Apollo, also painted inside the booth on the wall in front of him. Apollo's flat eyes stared into his own. The wide mouth a black hole he was meant to put his hand inside.

Judith swept back the curtain and leaned in, through the entranceway. She kissed his forehead, then swiped her credit card through the payment slot.

Scott stuck his hand into Apollo's mouth. Something jabbed his palm and he pulled his hand away. The machine whirred and a small slip of paper appeared from a slot to his right.

It was done.

He couldn't believe it was over so fast. He looked up at Judith, then down at the paper. He picked it up and turned it over. Some blood from his palm soaked into its white edge.

The paper said: *Judith*.

He stared at the word, his mind blank.

His first thought, when thoughts came, was to hide it from her. But he had held it out, unbelieving, for too long. She'd dropped the lingerie bag and staggered backwards. The curtain slung down to separate them. He crumpled the paper and rose, her name in his throat, but by the time he made his way out of the machine she was gone.

▼

HE DIDN'T KNOW WHAT TO DO so he shambled to the food court and sat down. He thought of nothing and after a while decided to go home.

He went to the parking lot and spent a long time looking for the car before he remembered they'd taken hers, then walked to the bus stop. When the bus came, he realized he didn't have the proper fare and overpaid with a five-dollar bill.

A little while after he sat down he realized he still held the piece of paper. He smoothed it out. It still said *Judith*, a smear of blood at the bottom of the *h* from where the needle had pricked him. Somehow, he'd thought it would say something different.

He shoved the paper between the cracks of the seat when the bus reached his stop. Judith's car wasn't in the driveway and she wasn't in the house.

He didn't know what he was supposed to do now. The dishes were dirty so he did the dishes. Judith had been drinking a glass of orange juice and left it half-full on the counter, left it out like he kept telling her not to do. He moved to finish it and wash the glass but decided to put it in the fridge instead.

He tried to watch television but there was nothing worth watching on television. He went to the bedroom and saw that her clothes from yesterday were on the floor. He picked up the clothes and put them in the laundry hamper, then realized her new lingerie was still at the mall, in its bag beside the machine where she dropped it.

He thought about the lingerie and how good she'd look but it didn't excite him. He felt detached from the image, like he was looking at her picture in a magazine.

He began to read, a book she left on the nightstand. She didn't live with him but slept over most nights. The book was *Timeline* by Michael Crichton. He thought it might help him understand something he was having trouble understanding. It had waited here for him, it should offer some insight.

But it was not the book he needed at the moment, and it seemed shameful that nothing in his life, not even a book, had anything to say to him right now.

▼

THE NEXT DAY SCOTT CALLED the office to say there had been a death in the family and he would be taking some time off. He called in the morning before anyone arrived so he only had to talk to the machine. His manager called back but he didn't pick up the phone and didn't listen to the message. He ate breakfast and went back to bed.

He wanted to call Judith or maybe show up at her place unannounced but that seemed wrong somehow. Instead he left her alone.

He thought about what the machine might have meant. Would she cause some accident, make some mistake, which would somehow result in his death? Would she pass on some sickness, some disease she would survive but to which he would succumb? Would she murder him? It seemed insane. But the machines were never wrong.

They were mindless and vague, mysterious beyond belief. But they were never wrong.

He spent the week in limbo. In bed or wandering through the house. He didn't shower, afraid of missing her call.

He spent a lot of time cooking. Grand, five-course meals, more food than he could eat. It relaxed him, gave him something to do, instructions to follow. He filled the fridge with leftovers and listened for the phone.

Then she called.

"Judith?" His voice cracked. He hadn't spoken for days.

There was a pause, and then her. "Scott?"

"Judith, come over."

"No." Her voice soft. "But I'd like to see you."

▼

SCOTT ARRIVED AT THE CAFÉ before her and turned the pages of *Timeline*. He'd brought the book to kill time and because he thought she might want it back. She could never start a new book until she'd finished the last one, and who knew when she would return to his house?

He wondered about the wedding and whether the wedding was off. He was thinking about this when she arrived and it showed on his face.

"Don't." She sat without saying hello. "What are we going to do?"

"We don't need to do anything. It's just your name. It changes nothing."

"It's not just my name." She was wearing her sunglasses indoors but he could still see her eyes. They crinkled at the corners as she fought to stay composed. "It means I'm going to kill you."

"It doesn't need to be so dramatic." He wanted to take her hand but thought it might make her more anxious. "Maybe you catch a cold, and I catch it too. When we're old. Maybe you lose control of a car. It doesn't mean you'll grow to hate me and poison my food."

"I suppose so." She swirled the coffee he'd ordered for her. She'd arrived late and it was cold. "But somehow I'm responsible."

"It doesn't matter. We don't need to do anything drastic. It's like you said: it's shocking, but something we need to accept."

"I can't accept this." She sipped her coffee and grimaced. "I just can't."

"If the machines are never wrong, then there's nothing we can do. We just have to keep living our lives, like we were before."

"You don't get it." She fumbled for her cigarettes, even though it was illegal to smoke indoors. "I can't accept it. And

I can't go on like before. It's like the buses. I know that it's pointless not to take the bus. No matter what, one day the bus will hit me when I'm walking, or driving, or whatever. Somehow, a bus will end up killing me. Whether I ride the buses or not. So why not ride them?"

"It might not mean that. Maybe someone name James Bus is going to hit you with his car. And maybe it means somebody else named Judith. You're not the only Judith."

She was quiet, playing with her cigarette.

He handed her the book. "I thought you might want to finish this."

She looked at the book like it was a UFO, something she'd never seen before and never expected to see. But then she took it. "Thanks."

"Look, you don't need to decide anything now. Let's just have coffee."

She nodded. "I suppose it could be someone else."

"Let me order you some new coffee. And a piece of cheesecake. We don't have to talk about it anymore if you don't want to, we can just talk. Think about it some more, but don't jump to conclusions."

"Okay. But just the cheesecake. I don't need more coffee, I'm jumpy enough."

He smiled. "There's a long line, I'll order while you have your cigarette." He moved to the counter and she went outside.

When his turn came he picked out the biggest piece of cake, the one that would take her the longest to finish. He motioned through the window for her to come back inside. She held up a finger and pulled hard on the cigarette while he looked at the cover of her Crichton book, thinking about the story so far.

▼

THEY RELAXED A LITTLE and talked until the cheesecake was gone, careful not to discuss the machine's prediction. It reminded him of their first date, tentative and awkward.

When she said she wanted to go home he didn't argue. "Can I walk with you?"

"Not today." She pulled herself into her coat.

They left together and she pulled out another cigarette. She was chain-smoking, which he hated to see, but he said nothing.

They stood outside for a while, looking at each other and looking away. She sniffed at the cold air.

He scanned her face. "It was good to see you. Call me later, okay?"

"Okay." She gave him a sad smile, but it was still a smile, so he took it. She turned and stepped into the street.

▼

SOMETHING HIT JUDITH HARD THEN, slamming into her back. She fell forward, gasping, breath slammed out onto the pavement.

A loud thud and screaming, screaming and the sound of brakes.

She lay in the street. Someone asked if she was hurt but she didn't answer.

▼

THE MACHINES WERE NEVER WRONG. Never wrong. But, dying, he wondered if he beat them.

Was that the bus? Had he saved her? The machines were never wrong, but maybe he saved her. Or would it happen again? Someday, in a future without him, when he couldn't push her out of the way?

Her book had fallen in the street. Her juice was still sitting in his fridge, which was full of food that was going to spoil.

Meals that he made for her. Judith.

THE DARK PART OF THE SKY

MY EARLIEST MEMORY IS OF SOCKS. My feet bare, my mother scolding. The socks were a day old, a present from my grandparents. A day old and already ruined, by my mother's standards. A mother's expectations are higher than a child could ever dream. It is a miracle that they continue to love.

The world is full of holes. They appear in socks, they eat through leaves, they arise in the ether itself, blossoming and elastic in the spaces between things. They flourish in our memories. The past is not the past at all, existing only in photographs and half-remembered, half-invented utterances.

The look on my mother's face. The trembling in her voice. Reality is threatening to consume itself, and with it, us. Bend your knees, say your prayers, beg forgiveness.

▼

SUNDAY MORNING, MOTHER AWAKENED my brother and me without fuss, breathing our names on the backs of our necks.

"David," she said. A fine mist, drifting down. I turned to her, eyes blurry with sleep, but she was already gone. Bending down to my sleeping brother on the lower bunk. "Joshua."

Even so early, she sported her Sunday best. "Come now. You can't sleep all day."

We longed to prove her wrong. I was the later riser, and lingered in bed while Joshua showered. I read. In those days, before the caterpillars came, I read young adult mysteries. The books had simple plots, money stolen or scammed. The criminals were clever, but not as clever as the young detective. Near the end of each book, our hero revealed the circumstances and motivations surrounding the commission of the crime. Once proved guilty through these logical manoeuvres, the criminals shrugged their shoulders and admitted defeat. They never tried to escape, appeal, or deny the charges.

Even so young, I was a skeptic. But I found these stories comforting. I liked thinking there were mysteries in the world—mysteries that could be solved, shelved, and moved beyond.

After breakfast, Mother went out to start the car while we hugged Father goodbye. Father never came to church. Neither of us asked why, since it seemed obvious. Church was the House of God, to which we paid weekly visits. Our home was the House of Father. It was only proper for each deity to maintain his own residence. I dipped my fingers in the font and crossed myself before God welcomed me into His house, and when I arrived home I knocked three times on the locked door and waited. There was silence. Then the staccato drumming of Father's long fingers, as if wondering whether to open the door, followed by a hard rap and the click of the door unlocking. All people and all places have their rituals.

I liked the *mystery* of church, that word the priest always used when he talked about God. He told the most strange and wonderful stories, of transformation, of miracles. When the caterpillars came, he spoke of plague. He always attempted to explain the meaning of these stories, and it was then that I struggled to sit still, keep my eyes open, stifle yawns. These explanations did not satisfy me. God was not a mystery like the ones in the books I read, something that could be explained away by connecting a few dots.

But if God was, indeed, a mystery, then He could be solved, explained. It was clear the priest believed this, but his conclusions seemed too reductive, he ignored large parts of the stories to focus on other, smaller parts. Mother echoed him, so was no help. My brother was nine, almost two years younger than me, and found it impossible to pay attention to anything, even God, for over half an hour. But Father, by not attending church, signalled to me that he had already solved this mystery.

However, he avoided the subject. Whenever I asked him questions, the room grew quiet. "Ask your mother," he said, but she was the one who had stopped speaking.

▼

THE CATERPILLARS TRICKLED INTO THE WORLD, a few tears preceding the flood. That spring, as I approached my eleventh birthday, I began to notice webbing in the trees. One night, while Father was eating a late dinner after a long day working at his brother's sawmill, I told him about these odd clumps of webbing. He stopped eating, put down his plate, moved to the doorway, and began putting on his shoes. "Show me."

I looked at Mother, but she looked away, and began to run water for the dishes. I pulled on my shoes while Father rummaged in the laundry room for a can of bug killer, and then led him to one of the small trees planted to screen off our yard from the neighbours.

"Up there." A small clump of webbing stretched from the trunk across three branches. Father took a long look, shook up the can, and sprayed the webbing until it dripped.

From then on, Joshua and I were my father's soldiers, on the hunt for tent caterpillars and their "camps." Father called them "army worms," and we took to calling them worms too, though we didn't draw the word out with the venom that he did. Our time playing in the town became more serious, and wherever we went we investigated the trees before beginning our games. Anything we found was reported to Father that night over dinner.

He was fanatical in his hunt, emptying can after can, but must have known from the beginning that he was fighting a losing battle. With each nest he demolished, his resolve diminished instead of increasing, hope fading in the face of hopelessness. When the town awoke one day to find it was being eaten alive, he didn't raise a single eyebrow in surprise. Instead, he walked through the house, closing all of the blinds—an oracle whose prophecy had come to pass, no longer in need of its vision.

Caterpillars clogged the streets. They caused accidents by obscuring road signs. They ruined footwear, guts soaking into the material, which cracked amber flakes and smelled like rotten meat. They stripped trees of their leaves, of their essence. The hunger of the worms was exceeded only by their number. Hundreds died every day, rose again in the night. They crawled into every conversation. *The worst it's ever been. An epidemic.*

Bold enough to invade my dreams, nighttime phantasms of zombie caterpillars crept over my skin. One night I woke shivering from such a nightmare, only to find myself face-to-face with one of the infernal worms. My father had failed. The world was no longer safe.

▼

I BEGAN WRITING THEN. It started as an offshoot of my reading, as I put away my simple mysteries in the face of more complex ones. I dug out the set of encyclopedias my parents had bought for me a few years ago, which they found at a garage sale and thought I could use when I started high school. It occurred to me that I knew nothing about the caterpillars, and that if I learned more about them I might be able to think of some way to deal with them. While reading, I found one entry suggesting another, and as I leapt from volume to volume I found it difficult to remember all the things I was learning. So I got my mother to buy me a small spiral-bound scribbler, where I recorded facts and bits of trivia about the caterpillars, and anything else I found interesting.

Even after the caterpillars were gone, I read and wrote until the notebook was full and I needed a second one. Just before starting this second book, I became interested in astronomy, fascinated by the idea of Earth as a small sphere amongst other spheres, something never discussed in church. This second book I divided into two sections. In the first I noted various bits of trivia. The second was reserved for definitions.

I liked astronomy because the words held such power. Among them were the names of gods, and simple gods at that, pinned to the sky in constellations like dead moths in display cases. These gods held no mystery. They offered their bodies to me, exposed themselves to every light. They were immense, and strange, but not unimaginable like the God who was both one and three.

It was not until many years later, while in university, that I stumbled upon my most interesting bit of trivia. In the centre of the Milky Way galaxy, at the heart of our small section of the universe, lies a supermassive black hole known as Sagittarius A*. At the centre of this black hole, like all others, exists a singularity, a point of compressed matter so dense that its gravity collapses all nearby matter and light into itself. This singularity is incredibly small, almost infinitely so, though it contains a mass estimated at 4.1 million times that of the sun. The majority of the expansive Sagittarius A* is a void in which nothing can exist without being drawn into the singularity. Once anything moves within the proximity of the black hole, passing a point of no return, it is absorbed.

Or so the theory goes. All science is theory, something that frustrated me as a child, but that I made my peace with later. Another theory I found fascinating was that of the Big Crunch. After time inestimable, the universe will collapse into itself. Worlds will collide. Galaxies will merge. Presence will be absence, the cosmos will be void, save for a sort of universal singularity, a dense point containing all energy and matter.

Every drop of rain, every beam of light, every word ever spoken, every once-living cell, all will become one. But only for an instant. The moment such perfect unity is achieved, a critical mass will be reached, and in one Big Bang the universe will rise, phoenix-like—as it has perhaps already done.

But this is only one possibility. The Big Crunch can only take place if there is sufficient matter present in the universe. Scientists have no accurate way to measure all the matter in the universe, but attempts to do so suggest that in fact there will be no Big Crunch after all. The alternate possibility is that the universe will continue to expand, dying a slow heat death as it does, slowing to a crawl and then a final, cold, and silent stop.

If these measurements are correct, our only hope for renewal lies in the existence of dark matter. Theorists are divided on the subject of its existence. Just as I wonder about the spaces between the stars: what lies there, in the dark part of the sky?

▼

IT WAS MIDDAY, and the sun blazed, but the curtain was drawn over the lone window in the room I shared with my brother. I used to like to look out at the sky, and let in the breeze, but I kept the window shut and drawn all the time now. The worms had suction-cup feet. They clung to the glass, writhed across its flatness. If you dropped them in water, they skipped across the surface tension to safety. Unholy soldiers, marching in mockery of the once-Lord Jesus.

They called to me in my dreams. *Come out amongst the waves. Outside. You will not drown, as long as you have faith.* I stayed seated inside. I was almost eleven, too old for miracles.

I read encyclopedias, my new Bibles. The door creaked. My breath stopped. I raised a book, to bring it down upon any fuzzy intruder. But it was only Joshua, and I began to breathe again.

"What are you doing?" Joshua's hands were pulled inside his sleeves.

"Reading. You?"

"Nothing." He shrugged into a chair. "I'm sick of these stupid caterpillars. I want to go outside."

"Then go outside."

"It's disgusting."

"I've been reading about these things. *Malacosoma disstria.*" I liked the hiss of the Latin. "There's a different kind in parts of the US, and if pregnant horses eat them the baby dies."

"I wish they would die."

"They will, if it gets cold."

"It won't get cold for months. After school starts."

Joshua swung his feet, bored. Waiting for me to think of a diversion. But I was not in the mood for diversions. I wanted solutions. I sat on the edge of the bed, looking into the darkness of the heating vent in the floor below. And somehow, from somewhere terrible, something rose.

"Come on," I said, stepping down from the bed.

"Come where?"

"I'll show you." I left the room and Joshua followed. I led him to the master bedroom. Father had gone to the sawmill and Mother was out shopping, but still we walked on our toes.

I rifled through their nightstands, pulling a pack of matches out of the drawer, a relic from Father's days as a smoker.

"What are you doing?"

"Just get dressed. We're going outside."

Joshua balked. "This is the dumbest idea ever."

"I haven't told you the idea yet."

"I don't care."

"Put on your boots. You might want to wear a jacket too, in case they start jumping from the roof."

"No." He stood in the hallway while I pulled on my rubber boats. "I'm not going."

"I need your help." I didn't, but it felt important, somehow, that he be with me. "Do you want to get rid of these things or not?"

Joshua looked down. "I guess so."

"Then get dressed. Better put on some gloves too."

▼

BUNDLED AND SWEATING, we lingered in the hallway for a while before getting up the nerve to open the door. Caterpillars exploded into my vision. The trees swayed beneath squirming waves of worms.

They walked in sheets across the lawn, stepping over one another in the search for food. Some were balled together, worm on worm, as if so ravenous they had resorted to cannibalism. My heart sank. How could the two of us be any match against the demons? They were legion.

"Follow me," I said. Steeling myself, I began to walk toward the garage, a separate building on our mid-sized lot. I turned back to Joshua, who still stood in the doorway. "What are you waiting for?"

"The garage is the worst place of all. They're raining off of it." The largest of the trees lining our yard hung over the building. Caterpillars fell from the tree in a visible torrent, onto the building and down to the ground.

"We'll run in, really fast. There aren't many in the building itself. Pull your jacket over your head." I glanced down to see caterpillars crawling up my boots. "Hurry."

I pulled my own jacket up over my head and ran toward the garage. This time, when I looked back, Joshua was following me. Caterpillars squelched beneath us. Their clinging corpses made our feet heavy and their innards made our footing treacherous, but we managed to reach the garage without tripping or falling.

Once safe inside the building, we inspected each other's jackets for caterpillars, flicking them away with our fingers. Along the back wall was a row of jars, filled with different types of nails and screws. I unscrewed one of the jars, dumped its contents onto a neat pile on the ground, and handed the jar to Joshua.

"We're going to empty all these jars," I said, "and then we're going to fill them with caterpillars."

He nodded and began emptying the jars. Not asking what we were going to do next, after the jars were full. Thankfully. I was afraid he would ask, not what but why. That was a question it seemed wrong to answer. I had ideas, but not reasons.

I still do not have reasons. When you are young, you do not need a reason for anything. You think of things, and then you do them. Some things make your parents smile, and some make the devil proud.

▼

WE SPENT THE NEXT HOUR repeating our actions. Jars were filled, matches struck, and fire dropped onto the unsuspecting caterpillars. They burned quicker than I thought they would. Thin wisps of black smoke, smelling of chlorophyll, rose from their bubbling, popping bodies. In death, the worms coalesced into a single molten mass. The sludge coated the jar, growing thicker and blacker. Their bodies fell away, melting together, so many collapsing into one.

I don't know how many of the caterpillars we managed to kill before our mother came home. She didn't scream, so we didn't notice her at first. She'd left the car running near the house and come looking for us, to help with her shopping bags. I heard Joshua draw a sharp breath, and turned to see him facing Mother, who stood near the garage door, silent and staring.

She looked broken, like a beaten dog. I hurried to snuff out the burning caterpillars, as if to erase them. She stood in the doorway for what seemed like a long time, eyes moving from jar to jar, moving over us, unable to rest on any particular thing.

I turned my back to her, to see what she was seeing: a row of jars, laid out with cold precision, and inside each a smouldering black mass no longer recognizable as ever having lived. A single jar held the next batch of victims, a horde of suffocating worms, climbing the walls in a futile attempt to escape. Their desperation was palpable, a stench as strong as the odour that rose from their burning bodies. Maddened, they crawled up the smooth glass only to fall back, and began to climb again with renewed fury.

In the jar I had just snuffed out, a few still-living caterpillars were mired in the sticky blackness, struggling against gelled corpses, to tear themselves loose from a death they had never before known.

I was saddened then by what I had done, but it was only when I turned to see Joshua, matches in hand, that I began to feel what my mother must have felt.

▼

I WAS QUIET AFTERWARD, as I am now. I thought about worms then, but now I think about black holes, of the void at the heart of the world. And I tapped my chest then, as I tap it still, like I used to knock on my father's front door.

When the gods died, they went up into the sky, but they couldn't fill it. The emptiness clung to the stars, multiplied between them, and keeps forcing them farther and farther apart. As they move out, away from each other and from parts of themselves, they slow down, grow tired and cold.

And they were gods. What will happen to me? Already, in my chest, I can hear it thud hollow.

GEORGE AND GRACIE

PHYSICS OFFERS NO CERTAINTIES. Gracie believes this. But if she could shrink down, could shrink small enough, then belief would not be necessary. She could see. At the quantum level, all is probability. And thus, upwards.

Chances are she will never walk through a wall, but this remains to be seen. The book she reads admits the possibility. If she walked against the wall for trillions of years, if she never died, if she chose to spend her immortality testing this theory, then one day she might blink, might open her eyes to find herself on the other side, in a world that all her life she has struggled to imagine.

▼

GRACIE HATES HER DREAMS. They confuse her, for they are not about anything. Just tones and colours, geometric shapes, chaotic patterns interrupting a uniform blackness. She can make no sense out of the visions and does not know why they frighten her. She wakes in the night, clammy and cold.

She turns to look at George.

His eyes stare, no longer asleep. Something awakened him in the night, some sound or pain. He is cold to the touch.

Gracie tests his pulse to be sure, even though she is already sure. She is a scientific woman, at heart.

George has been sick. Gracie closes and opens her eyes, over and over, hoping this is another dream. The kind of nightmare she expects. The kind that is almost comforting, that will mist away in the morning sun. She opens and closes her eyes, but when her eyes are open all she sees are George's eyes, vacant, and their reflection of her own.

When her eyes are closed she imagines. Other probabilities. Possible worlds.

▼

GEORGE SLEEPS AND SLEEPS, he is so tired these days. At first, Gracie goes to bed with him. She lies awake until he drifts away, staring at nothing, in absolute darkness. She used to work on film crews, in the lighting department, and now uses film blacking and other light-dampening material stolen from movies-of-the-week to seal the room, so that it is pitch black even in the middle of the day.

But Gracie can only pretend to sleep for so long. Cannot relax while listening to George's wet lungs. She sneaks away, into the light of the rest of the house, and finds quiet things to occupy her time. For a while, she watched movies, the volume low, but she can't watch movies anymore. They make her want to go back to work, and she can't go back to work, not when George needs her here.

So, she reads. She has never been much of a reader, but makes her way through George's small library in less than a month. Then she starts to compile her own library. She orders books online while George sleeps. E-mails the writers, directors, and producers she knows, who are always scavenging the planet for "content," and has them recommend books.

Gracie ends up reading non-fiction for the most part, since audiences love true stories. One day, a friend who makes documentaries recommends a popular science book, *The Elegant Universe* by Brian Greene. When her friend describes the book, it sounds boring, physics at its most speculative. But Gracie trusts her friend's taste, and orders it.

▼

GEORGE AND GRACIE drive home from the hospital. Everything is in remission and George feels good. He asks to drive. There is no reason why he can't drive, the doctor made this clear, but still it makes Gracie nervous. But he begs, so they switch seats when she stops for gas.

George has the radio on and sings along. He can't sing and knows it, tries to compensate with enthusiasm. He's the happiest he's been in months. Gracie's nervousness melts and she even joins in for a few choruses.

The car is hit on the driver's side. A loud noise and the world shifts. Gracie's head strikes glass and her eyes close. When they open again, someone tells her that a truck ran a red light and George was killed on impact. She closes her eyes again and when she opens them next the only difference is that things are a little less blurry.

▼

THE BOOK IS GREENE'S ATTEMPT to popularize difficult concepts regarding string theory, a branch of theoretical physics. It's a hard book for Gracie to read because the world the theory describes is so counter-intuitive. Even the beginning of the book, which discusses established and more familiar concepts like general relativity and quantum mechanics, offers notions foreign to her way of thinking.

As a child, she found it difficult to imagine the Earth as round, something that extended beyond her vision. Even now, it is hard for her to believe that George is still in the house. She has to suppress the urge to run into the bedroom, hold open the door and let in the light, verify that their marriage and his sickness aren't just dreams.

But even though she finds the ideas difficult, they intrigue her. It's freeing to think that the world isn't what she believes it to be.

▼

GEORGE WAKES FOR LUNCH. She makes tomato soup, his favourite, and a sandwich with avocado, cheese, and turkey. She also makes chicken noodle soup for herself, since she hates tomato. George has an appetite today and wants to eat outside so they sit on the porch and talk about books.

George is reading Italo Calvino's *If on a winter's night a traveller*, which an experimental filmmaker recommended and Gracie already finished. He loves the book, loves Calvino's obvious joy, but is having trouble following the story. Reading tires him and sometimes he has to reread whole chapters.

Gracie tries to tell him about Greene's book but she can't quite put the concepts into words. She has a hard time understanding them herself and George keeps asking questions she can't answer. However, they both latch onto the notion that everything travels at the speed of light at all times, only this travel is expended both through the world and through time. Light does not age, travelling through space but not time, and the faster one moves the slower one ages, relatively speaking. At least, this is how Gracie understands the concept.

George loves the idea that while he is lying still in bed, lamp off, too tired to even read, he is travelling through time near the speed of light. He gets excited when he talks about it. And, as he talks, thin cracks begin to appear in his skin.

The cracks widen as George smiles and wonders about the marathon through time that he is running at this very moment, when he finds it difficult to even stand for long. Light begins to spill from the cracks as they widen. Soon they are wider than Gracie's fingers. She's startled and moves toward George, who is still talking, oblivious.

She tries to take George into her arms, hold him together, but the cracks are so wide now that her hands and arms fall into them and George comes apart. He comes apart and falls to the ground in pieces that spool away in steady trails of light.

Until his eyes vanish they remain wide, with wonder at his newfound world.

▼

WHAT GRACIE FINDS MOST INTERESTING about string theory is the notion of parallel universes. This is a well-worn idea, the subject of countless lousy movies. But the idea that other universes could be a physical possibility, not just an act of the imagination, startles and excites her.

She has just a hazy notion of what "parallel universes" might mean, to a physicist. But it seems like it might mean actual other universes, different worlds with different physical laws, where what might seem impossible in this world is common, even banal. And how many other worlds could there be? There might be any number, an infinite number.

If there could be an infinite number of universes, then it would stand to reason that anything she could imagine, the contents of every movie she'd ever worked on and every book she'd ever read, would have happened somewhere in the multiverse. She's not sure if this is an accurate picture of the cosmos, but even if she doesn't understand string theory or its implications, well, it doesn't seem like anybody else does, even the experts. She flips to the index, looks up any mention of the multiverse or parallel universes and rereads those pages. She wants so much for these things to be true.

▼

GEORGE COMES OUT of the bedroom while Gracie is reading. "I'm feeling much better," he says. "I mean, I feel great." His smile is wide and bright. "Really wonderful." Head to toe, he is a mass of blood.

His skin has abandoned him and he's now just exposed bone, blood, and muscle. The fat fell off long ago. His lips are gone. Teeth bared in a horrid grin.

"I think I'd like to go out for dinner tonight." George collapses onto the living room carpet. The blood stains and spreads. Gracie watches all of this without moving, without a word. There is nothing in her anymore.

▼

IN ONE PART OF GREENE'S BOOK, where he's trying to explain the principle of relativity, Greene asks the reader to imagine two figures, whom he names George and Gracie, both travelling through space.

The naming is a horrible coincidence. Gracie wants to close the book, but can't. *Imagine*, Greene asks.

Imagine that George, who is wearing a spacesuit with a small, red flashing light, is floating in the absolute darkness of completely empty space, far away from any planets, stars, or galaxies. From George's perspective, he is completely station-

ary, engulfed in the uniform, still blackness of the cosmos. Off in the distance, George catches sight of a tiny, green flashing light that appears to be coming closer and closer. Finally, it gets close enough for George to see that the light is attached to the spacesuit of another space-dweller, Gracie, who is slowly floating by. She waves as she passes, as does George, and she recedes into the distance. This story can be told with equal validity from Gracie's perspective. It begins in the same manner with Gracie completely alone in the immense still darkness of outer space. Off in the distance, Gracie sees a red flashing light, which appears to be coming closer and closer. Finally, it gets close enough for Gracie to see that it is attached to the spacesuit of another being, George, who is slowly floating by. He waves as he passes, as does Gracie, and he recedes into the distance.

Gracie reads and rereads this, and cries. In none of her dreams, when she is frightened without knowing why, does she cry, and in none of her visions of George's death, terrible fantasies which refuse to leave her, does she shed a single tear. But she cries now.

She cries thinking of the two of them, in space, each believing that they are still and that it is the *other* who is moving, coming close and then floating away. Each of them waving, wanting to reach out and take hold of the other. Wanting to know why the other won't stop. Why they wave and just keep going.

▼

GEORGE COLD TO THE TOUCH. Gracie tests his pulse to be sure, even though she is already sure. She is a scientific woman, at heart.

She doesn't cry.

Instead, she goes into the bathroom and begins to swallow pills. She slumps to the floor, head back against the base of the sink, trying to pace herself, not wanting to throw them up.

She thinks of all the possible worlds there might be, worlds she cannot imagine. Perhaps somewhere, in one of those worlds, exists a happier ending to this story.

SHE TURNS THE PAGE and the lights go out. Aleya plunges into the night's stomach. Into the whale. Where she will be either digested or transformed.

She puts the book down, on the back of the couch. She has been pacing and reading, pacing and reading, from the kitchen to the couch, and when the lights go out she stops mid-stride. Seeks the microwave clock: dead. The power then, not just the bulbs. She doesn't have a flashlight. Her father always kept one on top of the fridge, checked its batteries every week. When he died, she thrust it away, into a box somewhere, not able to bear the sight of it each day.

In the darkness, her eyes are drawn to the window. A strange brightness trickles in through the pane. Impossibly, she can see *more* than when outside, out on the porch, when the street lights and house lights still glowed.

▼

OUTSIDE, EVERYTHING'S SILENT as well as dark, even more quiet than before. Neither the whir of the night nor the dial tone of traffic. Just the creak of the porch under her. The hand of some god has swept this table clean.

She should stay here. Go back inside, go to sleep. Let morning correct this. Let the sun rise to redraw the day.

But she knows she cannot. Feels the pull of some cord, wrapped tight around her waist. Drawing her away, to the river. Drawing her closer, but to what?

Edged in terror, she steps down the street. The dead street. Not a breeze stirs even a leaf, although they crackle underneath her socked feet. She's neglected her shoes, neglected her safety, to step into this nightmare of darkness.

She expects another face. To meet someone on this street, in this night. To share this night, its sudden cold. Someone else must feel this pull. But nothing but shadows, nothing even in the shadows. Her breath the one sign of any life.

Her breath, visible in the air before her. The summer night cold as late autumn. No wonder she cannot get warm. She wishes for a sweater, thinks to turn back for one, but cannot. Aleya pants her way down to the river.

Only to find that the river is gone.

Impossible. The river is gone.

In its place lies an ocean. Endless water. The city that should continue on the other bank has disappeared or drowned.

This must be a dream. Yes. All a dream, like she at first wanted. Like she wished. It has all been a dream. None of it was real. Aleya didn't meet a writer in her tea shop. He didn't leave a book. There never was a tea shop. Her parents run a bookstore, remember? Her parents never died.

The darkness total, but she can still see. Some light glows from somewhere. As if moonlight washed across the land, down onto the waves. But when she looks up she sees no moon. There are no stars.

▼

HER MOUTH OPENS IN THE DEAD NIGHT. Out of Aleya drift words, but not her words. Words she once read. "We live on a placid island of ignorance in the midst of black seas of infinity, and it was not meant that we should voyage far."

Then silence. The words tumble into this sea, dissolve. Before her, the black water stretches. Behind her, the old world.

Aleya's body starts to shake. She's stopped moving long enough for the fear to catch up with her. She gasps, trembles. Her left hand spasms open. Somehow, without realizing it, she still carries the book. Although she swears that she did not, a moment ago. She swears she left it in her house. Yet she holds it now, in a death grip. Grasps it mindless above this strange shore.

Then she drops the books, spasms it away, as if she just now noticed she held a live snake.

The book falls into the water. Splashes and bobs.

Then the water starts to transform to ice.

Aleya shakes and stares, as this ocean, this black sea, freezes over. Crystal by crystal, crackling. A shockwave spread from the dropped book.

THE NIGHTMARE BALLAD OF
THE DRUNKEN BRAND IDENTITY
WITH A CAMEO BY SHAKESPEARE
AND A TITLE THAT CANNOT GET WORSE

THE NIGHTMARE BEGINS when you look at a gun. This is how it always begins. Then the gun comes over to ask what you're looking at and you say *Nothing*, then look down in your drink. Then the gun smiles, recognizing you as its old friend.

Then death happens and the nightmare begins, or maybe has already begun before death happens and death is just part of the nightmare. Life is the nightmare and death is the nightmare and both keep happening and neither matters now, neither matters in the face of the nightmare.

Maybe in the moment they seem significant. But soon they just become normal, things that happen. Soon your body's shoved aside for the next one.

▼

YOUR BODY, UNWANTED, slinks out of the bar, slinks down the street. In the street it wants somewhere to lie but everything is walls or hydrants or just other bodies in the night wind. In the street, people talk to your body and their faces are the new face of the nightmare.

"Hey."

Your body won't arrest itself for one word.

"Hey!"

Your body won't—

"Hey-yo, Daddy-O!"

Your body slows. Turns back. Checks its watch. The day had been going so well. Two-eighteen in the afternoon and you hadn't remembered being alive once.

"Hey, you want me to suck your dick?"

Alone with her, near an alley, a bit back from the street.

"Hey! You want me to suck your dick, or what?"

You look off into the alley, then back at her. She bites her bottom lip, smearing the red a little down her pale chin. She seems too young. She's playing at this.

"Yes, but I'll say no."

She pulls her teeth into her mouth and nods at your sage wisdom. Then her lip comes up in a snarl. "What's your fucking story?"

▼

WHAT, INDEED? BACK at the office after lunch at the bar, head blown apart by the morning's gun, you ponder her question. What *is* your fucking story?

What's its point? What are the intentions of its author? When you are drunk you imagine yourself in a story and you are drunk all the time now.

Who is your author? What is his motivation? He insisted on years of growth and change, decades of struggle were for some reason required. So that you could sit in a yellow boardroom? In an office in Ottawa, near the seat of the nation's power? And instead of revolution, instead of marching forth for change, you could sit at this long fake-wood table and brainstorm ways to utilize social media to grow your brand's tribe and leverage influence as a thought leader

124

in the niche market for marshmallows that can somehow be used during sex.

"Kids these days are having lots of sex. How can we convince them that marshmallows would help them have more and more exciting sex, when they are already sexing in ways unknown to all previous generations?"

You don't have an answer so you nod as if you did, but the answer needs a few more minutes to bake. You stare at the shitty yellow wall. Is this yellow wallpaper an allusion to "The Yellow Wallpaper" by Charlotte Perkins Gilman?

Why not? Your life is a horror story, you're losing your fucking mind.

You're starting to get on a drunken roll, nodding like your neck might break as your mind bakes your fake ideas. Then Bob from marketing fucks it all up by opening his stupid fucking mouth.

"Why don't we try to utilize social media to grow our brand's tribe and leverage influence as a thought leader?"

"Good idea, Bob!"

You nod as if you agree with Bob but your agreement just needs a few more minutes to bake.

You stare at Bob's neck and imagine pushing a knife through its soft flesh. Finding some way to balance the knife between his shoulder and neck just right. If you balanced the knife just right it wouldn't cut his throat unless he moved wrong and then it would be his fault really. You just put the knife there and walked away before the damage was done. You gave it to him for safekeeping but then the idiot moved and anyway you see really he's the one that moved. You'd be blameless and not held to account in a court of law.

▼

NEXT HE SEES, and notice the shift here to the third person, he sees himself like he is outside of his body, a reader of this lousy story he's also in, he sees himself volunteering to lead a task force dedicated to whatever the hell Bob just said.

And he does not know what this guy is thinking, this half-drunk or maybe full-drunk idiot, what the hell is he thinking volunteering to lead this task force?

Who even mentioned a task force?

He did, apparently, he came up with the idea of a task force. Whatever that is, either a mission for GI Joe or a bull-shit work committee led by some jackass. Which will it be? Only time will tell, as Shakespeare didn't say, though it sounds like something he would say. *Time shall unfold what plighted cunning hides, / Who covers faults at last with shame derides.* Cordelia to her sisters. The good child to the bad. This drunk jackass knows his literature at least.

He knows his literature and he knows how to drink himself stupid over the lunch hour and get back to the office late and barely make it to the meeting. He knows a lot of stuff, it's true, and yet he can't get it together to refer to himself in the first person.

At least he manages to cut Bob out of the task force.

The day is already a nightmare, we've established that, so let's just forget about it, let's skip it, skip skip to the evening. In the evening he sits at home alone and doesn't mind being alone but does start to think about that girl on the street.

He should have at least talked to her about the idea. It had promise. Kids these days have lots of good ideas. They start businesses before they hit puberty, have pop hits while still in high school. They make movies starring ice buckets and keep fashionable pets and overthrow dictators using #hashtags.

His company even hired two kids, two youth consultants, they want to consult with the youth so they pay two kids who are still in grade school twice what he gets paid because they seem like cool kids. They have skateboards that are like two skateboards attached by a string so that's cool, right? And it's even cooler when you are in grade school and approaching a six-figure salary and all you have to do is go to a meeting in a yellow boardroom for like two hours every three weeks. And you just text your friends while you're there because that's what they are paying you to do. If you stop texting your friends and start paying attention and ever get caught taking life seriously then you will be Facebooked a Donald Trump meme and that's how you'll know you've been fired.

Cool is YouTube or whatever's cool now, cool is how kids still say cool even though everything else is fleek or whatever, cool is Frankenstein's monster and how they all know it's not called Frankenstein but call it Frankenstein anyway, but they know. Oh, they know. Youth and cool, the divine sparks to the marketing monster.

Cool's like pornography, you know it when you see it. Some kids say maybe it's cool to question white privilege and maybe it's cool to be a feminist and to those kids the adults say um yeah sure but sorry you're not what we're looking for. Find some Meninist girl and give her the keys to this Mercedes. If Mercedes are still cool.

Kids are better than adults, everyone knows that, they just need some support, they need to be given money for not working and they need to be believed in like they are Jesus. Mercedes is what they called Jesus's mom in Spanish, by the by. It also means *wages* and *reward*, which somehow in Latin connects up to *pity*.

He could have helped that girl. With the right brand identity and a better value proposition she could found an empire.

▼

THE NEXT DAY his head splits because he was drinking at night too. Thinking about Shakespeare always leads to thinking about the human tragedy, and the tragic girl on the street didn't help, nor the missed opportunities of the day and of life, and thinking this way always drives him to drink.

Another drink to get the train moving.

The train moves and you are a *you* again, it doesn't always happen so you treasure it, and your homemade Irish coffee in a plastic Starbucks carrier is as always the perfect camouflage.

And you are happy again, whistling while you go to work in improbable imitation of someone who's not deep in a nightmare.

In your office you decide to write a poem. That seems like the logical first step—some creative brainstorming to figure out what the fuck you're going to do now that you have some idiotic ill-defined project to deliver that you put on your own plate and can't even complain about. Poetry is a time-honoured way to waste your life while drawing connections between ideas so you decide to drum up a stanza of four lines because for some reason you think all stanzas should be four lines.

~~Out your office window no scratch that~~ Out the window of the cafeteria table where you sometimes drink coffee and hide from co-workers while you think, you can spy the National Gallery of Canada. You decide to start there and then slide into the social branding shit.

You end up with this:

128

Let's install a food court in the National Gallery.
Like the hospital McDonald's it will nourish our soul.
Shakespeare remains an expert in the field of social branding.
As Milton tells us, Shakespeare's corpse has got it going on.

The poem has a certain charm and has you thinking about Shakespeare again and what he might still have to teach us today. Your favourite lines from Shakespeare come from *King Lear*:

I' th' last night's storm I such a fellow saw,
Which made me think a man a worm. My son
Came then into my mind, and yet my mind
Was then scarce friends with him. I have heard more since.
As flies to wanton boys are we to th' gods.
They kill us for their sport.

How dark and depraved a truth is this, and the man speaking just *saw* this storm happening to another person, just *saw* the torment, the torture, and it is as if he saw his future in this way, saw the steel come for his eyes.

King Lear is a play about torture and the truth of torture, how the truth of torture is that the world is a nightmare. The world is a nightmare in which the gods play. Where dudes fuck with one another and ruin everything they can reach.

Dudes are always fucking with other dudes in Shakespeare. Gouging out eyeballs and dipping swords in poison and making long speeches while they die about how dying is different from what they expected but still worthwhile and you should try it sometime.

Which reminds you Shakespeare invented the word *eyeball* although that was from *The Tempest* but anyway maybe this is the key, maybe marshmallows need some cool new name like *sexmallows* and that will get kids these days to fuck with marshmallows.

Have marsh sex with sexmallows or something. Invent some word shit like Shakespeare would. *If Shakespeare was fucking today, he'd have marsh sex with* SEXMALLOWS™. You're close to something, so close.

You're proud, you deserve a drink; hell, you've done so well that you deserve death.

▼

HE WAKES UP IN HIS ROOM AGAIN and it has been another day *since*, that makes two days *since*, he figures, the day the nightmare happened doesn't count because it was always happening, he just didn't see it, and also there is the word *since*, yesterday was one day after, so one day *since*.

Today is the second day since it happened, so what the fuck is he still doing waking up? What the fuck is he still doing walking around?

Why are you drinking your morning alcohol and bussing to your fucking job when everything already happened?

I need a name, you decide, maybe a name would help sort out all this *you/he* crap. What was your name before everything happened? It doesn't matter, you suppose, that name is gone.

You need a new name. Maybe *Bob*? But that name's already taken, by Bob, who walks into your office.

Bob has come to bitch about how you stole his idea and started the task force and then didn't let him be on the task force. "What's worse and more of an insult is that your task force just seems to be a list of fictitious names rather than

130

other employees you've wrangled. In fact, your task force looks a lot like the character list from *King Lear*."

You don't remember sending any memo. "That's ridiculous."

"I agree—it's ridiculous."

"Why would I copy out the character list from *King Lear* and distribute that as my task force roster?"

"I don't know. But this sure looks like the character list from *King Lear*." Bob turns the memo toward you.

> *To: Whom It May Concern*
> *From: Task Force Captain*
>
> *Subject: Task Force Member List (for reference)*
>
> *Captain*
> *Cordelia, daughter to Lear*
> *Curan, a courtier*
> *Doctor*
> *Duke of Albany*
> *Duke of Burgundy*
> *Duke of Cornwall*
> *Earl of Gloucester*
> *Earl of Kent*
> *Edgar, son of Gloucester*
> *Edmund, bastard son to Gloucester*
> *Fool*
> *Gentleman*
> *Goneril, daughter to Lear*
> *Herald*
> *King of France*
> *Knight*
> *Lear, King of Britain*

Messenger
Old Man, tenant to Gloucester
Oswald, steward to Goneril
Regan, daughter to Lear
Servant 1
Servant 2
Servant 3

cc: Bob

"Bob, why are you wasting my time with this shit?"

"Just let me on the task force. I will do all the work and you can take most of the credit. I just want, like, some of the credit."

"No dice. I refuse to budge an inch on this."

"You're not the only asshole that read Shakespeare. I know that he invented that phrase.'"

"Well, then we've come full circle."

"Why are you fucking with me?"

"Truth will out. The game is up."

"Quit it!"

"Bob, you're losing it. A task force memo that is just the cast list of *King Lear*? A conversation where I keep quoting Shakespeare just to be an asshole? It doesn't make sense. It's an improbable fiction."

"You know I have a PhD in Shakespeare, right? You must know. Is this your way of reminding me how my life sucks because I'm working at a fucking marshmallow company since the academic job market is shit? Why are you being such a jerk? What did I do to you?"

"Though this be madness, yet there is method in it." You stand and make a show of putting on your jacket, which you actually forgot to bring to work, so you just mime putting on a jacket.

"You didn't even try that time."

"Parting is such sweet sorrow." And with a little salute and a wave, you are out the door, leaving a sweaty Bob behind.

▼

THE MORE YOU THINK ABOUT IT, the more you seem trapped in an improbable fiction. The more it seems like your story means nothing and goes nowhere. The thought scares you because of everything that has happened, how the nightmare keeps happening to you. If the nightmare means nothing, that is worse somehow than the nightmare itself.

You want so much for it to mean something, for everything to have been things that happened and not just things that happen. There is the verb tense to consider. Things should be things that *happened* but they seem more and more like they *happen*, they keep *happening*, keep unfolding across the days.

You drink so much now and you thought that was because of what *happened* but maybe it's because it keeps *happening* and *happening* and never stops.

You need to reach a point where it *happened* and something else can *happen*. Even if that something else is nothing, nothingness and erasure. You would love erasure so much, love to be a thing erased.

If only you had been erased when your name was erased but instead you became a zombie, what happened in your apartment, in that room, what happened *happened* but you keep returning to its *happening*, you keep going toward it *happening again*.

Where is it all, where is it now? Bring death to me, you pray to the gods who kill.

Bring it to me, like a wanton fly I buzz from home to work to bar to bottle and to the body oh the body please take this body from me you pray.

▼

THREE DAYS NOW since it happened, seems symbolic enough, time to get things moving, time to get it all going for real, so you step into a gun store and step up to the gun store counter.

"Gimme a gun, I need to kill myself quick."

The clerk blinks and squints. "You can't just walk into a gun store and say something like that and expect to get a gun quick."

"Why the hell not?"

The man spits. "Permits."

"Goddamn."

"You don't need to tell me, buddy."

"Look, I gotta end this thing. Drinking yourself to death is too slow and requires too much storytelling. A gun would be nice and quick, you just need a motivation, and I'm the kind of character that pops his own head off with a gun so I don't even really need much in the way of that."

"I don't know what you're talking about, which is another reason I can't sell you a gun today."

"Shit. Well, I gotta go then."

▼

GOTTA GO, GOTTA RUN. Gotta get to work, there's a meeting, you're ready to unveil your new ad campaign, which we all assume will go over very well indeed.

Does your author even need to describe this meeting? It seems destined to go well, and thus be uneventful, so why even bother? Maybe he should just spend time describing something else.

Yes, just describe something else, Herr Author. Mein Author, don't bother with this boring meeting, just another ho-hum sort of meeting, nothing special, just gonna unveil the ad campaign that the task force has been developing, it should be pretty routine and just go over pretty well.

Maybe a few hitches, a few hitches probably since you didn't get a gun so that part of the plan went out the window, suicide by gun in the meeting would have been a fun way to conclude and also a good way to avoid the painful question period that always follows a presentation. But in Canada you need to wait for your guns, I guess, what the fuck?

Seems like we need a new system, call an election quick. I've gotta vote here ready to cast for the first guy that will give me a gun.

▼

YOUR AUTHOR'S NOT SURE what else to describe so he might as well write about the meeting, the boring ol' meeting about the task force ad plan unveiling, just a few boring ol' PowerPoint slides.

Slide one just says TASK FORCE PRESENTS AD CAMPAIGN FOR SEXMALLOWS MASTER PLAN CONCEPT all strung together like that and in all caps and italics like that too.

Slide two is a series of bullets:

- *marshmallows = boring*
- *sexmallows = sexy*
- *marsh sex = some sort of cool sex that uses sexmallows (leave it to the kids to figure this out)*
- *Shakespeare = successful brand leader*
- *brand rebranding with brand leadership as the brand goal*

Slide three is Shakespeare with his dick out getting a blowjob. You've collaged together a porn scene and a portrait of Shakespeare and also a big hand giving a thumbs up. It's all super graphic and disgusting and sure to get you fired.

"Any questions?"

Silence. Even the kids, the preteen youth consultants, have been shocked into silence.

You decide to take the silence as a good sign. "Well, we'll get started on this then."

You start repacking your briefcase, but your boss waves for you to wait. Waves his hand at you a few times, too many times, like he isn't sure what to say but knows he needs to say something.

Eventually he spits it out: "What the fuck is this?"

Good question. Your author is having second thoughts of this kind too. Has he gone too far? Can he really put this into a story?

What if his family reads it, what will they think? But it is too late for these questions, you suppose.

▼

ACTUALLY, THAT IS SOMETHING you say out loud. "It is too late for these questions."

"You want to run an ad campaign of Shakespeare getting his cock sucked?"

"Sure. I've always wanted that."

More silence. You wait a few more moments, then go back to packing up your briefcase.

The youth consultants have leaned forward to stare at the Shakespeare slide, which is still displayed. Like they never saw porn, or maybe never saw Shakespeare. For children brought in to help figure out how to convince other children to start having sex with marshmallows, they seem prudish.

Your boss's boss, the vice president of marketing, is here too, since it's such an important meeting. And because you sent her a personal invite that you handmade by cutting and pasting lines from your Oxford edition of *King Lear* so that it looked like a cross between a birthday card and a ransom note. She looks even more stunned than your boss.

She raises her hand, like this was high school.

"Yes?"

"Where's the marshmallow?"

You turn to consider the collage, as if seeing it for the first time. "Up his ass."

"You're fired."

"At this juncture, I'd like to thank Bob for all his help."

Bob chokes on his coffee. All eyes shift to him as you slip out of the room.

●   ▼

OMG YOU LAUGH to yourself on the bus ride home. OMG you can't believe that you did it. OMG, like the kids say.

O, M, and might I add G.

OMG kiddie cakes. You imagine Biblical stories unfolding in a beer commercial or something, your wife your dead wife, deadly beloved turns back to look for her daughter and then crumbles to a pillar of salt and you just say "OMG" and then smile and crack open a brewski.

Not to worry because the beer turns the haggard old crones fleeing the city with you into young bikini models, good timing with the wife dying/turned-to-salt thing. OMG.

OMG is what Mary Magdalene said when Jesus rose. *OMG WTF r u doing here? I thot death happened to u?*

137

OMG *that's so silly!* says Jesus, OMG *like whatevs death is no biggie.*

OMG *haha guess not haha.*

Jesus is like, *Lazarus! forgeddaboutit!!!!* and then Lazarus rises, up from the dead. Death is no biggie it just happens sometimes but Jesus is there to say fuck it forgeddabout death.

▼

HE FINISHES HIS DRINK but nothing happens. Nothing happens even though it already happened. What is he doing wrong?

He gets up and puts the glass down but misses the table and it shatters as it hits the hardwood. Splinters of glass slide themselves into his path and he cuts up his feet as he heads to the next room.

To the next room, the next room, the one with the corpse.

The smell has stopped bothering him. He sits down on the bed beside the corpse and lowers his hand to touch the corpse's leg. A gentle touch. Blood drains from his feet into the floorboards and he takes his hand off of the corpse.

"How did you do it?" The corpse says nothing.

"What did you do?" The corpse silent still.

He's out of ideas. He lies down on the bed, at the foot of the bed, at the feet of the three-day-old corpse. The corpse is small and huddled, its knees pulled into its chest, and there is still plenty of room on the bed.

"How did you make it happen? How did you get it to work?" He stares at the ceiling as he asks his child, his daughter the corpse who does not reply, does not even know he is here.

His daughter the corpse. OMG, o my god.

god o god, o my dear god o god.

o god no, please grant us this prayer.

WHILE YOU SLEEP I RECORD YOUR DREAMS

WHILE YOU SLEEP I record your dreams. My device so gentle it does not wake you. Its invisible waves caress your tired head, like a vampire might brush a fine neck.

Before you wake I shut down the device and remove it. This is why you do not know about my research. You will receive this letter later, when I am gone. When you are left alone with the device.

My project is complex and you will not understand. It takes a scientific mind like mine. This letter is intended to explain neither its scope nor its glory, but some of the effects that you have not yet noticed, but will suffer from soon. I write *suffer*, but you should not fear. We all suffer. Your suffering will be different, in that it will have purpose.

In this sense, you are lucky I chose you. I apologize for nothing and will be held to no account.

I write to you from the beginning stages. My gluttonous machine feeds, fills. Yet even when it is full, it will not be satisfied. At that point, it will begin to belch forth your dreams. And so, your old dreams will replace your new ones. You will find yourself in a loop, dreaming the same series, again and again, as the machine regurgitates your nighttime world.

As the nights pass, you will forget how to dream for yourself. Though it pales in comparison with my beautiful device, the human body is a machine as well. It will rust. When I am satisfied that you have forgotten everything, I will leave you. And leave with you this letter, this device.

You will have a choice to make then. Will you continue to dream your same dreams, or destroy the device and live a life without dreams? The results of either choice will be fascinating, as will the choice itself.

My tumour grows, so there is only time for this one, final experiment. My research into electrical fields has convinced me of another life, where I may not act but may be an observer. Which is why I will end this life. I must end it before the tumour grows.

I know that you hate me from reviewing your murderous dreams. But sacrifices are necessary. By the time you read this letter, I will have sacrificed myself, and in another way, I have sacrificed you. We are offerings to science. Take some solace in that. Your hatred has been hard to bear, but it is part of the experiment, so must be borne.

What I do I do out of love for this world, where everything hides. For what hides must be found and uncovered.

I will miss you but it is better this way, to keep the experiment pure and control my own end. There is a place where my mind is going, and I must halt its progress or compromise my conclusions. Know that although I am gone, I still watch you, my son.

I still watch, and I gather the data.

CAPITALISM

WE KNOW CAPITALISM hates mornings because he always forgets his travel mug and has to give his name at Starbucks. Capitalism bought the travel mug just to avoid this horror. Why he forgets the mug remains a mystery. He wakes at 4:00 a.m. and goes through a morning routine designed by a life consultant that takes over two hours, after which Capitalism brims with energy and ideas. You would think somewhere in there he would remember the mug. But he always forgets it, even though his mind is sharp, even though he never tires. He forgets it without fail, so has to give his name at Starbucks.

He cannot bear to give his real name, not to these energy vampires, so he offers some fake name, a different one each time. "Cary. Carmichael. Crane." He tries to have fun with it. "Johann. Job. Susan. Tripoli. Thor." He offers stranger and stranger names to blander and blander baristas. "Rumpelstiltskin. Rutabaga. Rin-Tin-Tin. Roger-Dodger. Rick Roll."

The baristas never react. They just write the name down.

Capitalism hates them. He considers a different coffeehouse, considers a Keurig, but who is he kidding? He's Capitalism. He goes to Starbucks every day, many times each day. Capitalism needs coffee. Sometimes, he gives three different names throughout the day, to the same person. Who just writes the name down.

The worst part, somehow, is not that nobody reacts. It's that nobody ever misspells Capitalism's fake name.

▼

WHEN CAPITALISM ARRIVES at the office on Monday, his coffee already gone, consumed in scalding flashes during a noisy commute, the hive already buzzes with news. Today, the buzz carries out to the parking lot. In an effort to increase employee engagement and jump on the latest management trend of "flattening the pyramid," the company is offering any employee an opportunity to have dinner with the CEO.

They don't want their pyramid too flat for too long, so are running a contest. Dinner is the prize, a five-course meal at a three-star restaurant, but the real prize is the dinner guest. Winner takes all: a private, intimate audience with the CEO, not to exceed two hours, during which he will listen to all thoughts, take all ideas under consideration. One hinted-at but not-guaranteed part of the prize is a possible promotion.

Buzz-buzz goes the office. Perhaps the winner will, if they manage to impress the CEO enough during this dinner, leapfrog over others. In a few short weeks, buzzes the hive, in a few days, overnight, maybe somebody could pop into a position that might otherwise take a decade to attain.

To enter the company contest, you simply offer a one-page proposal (the guidelines for that single page's margins, font and font size, and other formatting runs for seven pages). This proposal may present only a single idea, an idea so brilliant in concept that it can be clearly and concisely stated on that single page yet return a mountain of value—nay, a mountain range.

The deadline is Friday. Any employee can enter, whether they work in the lobby, mailroom, boiler room, or boardroom.

"In other words." Sara loves to say, *In other words*, then stop, as if that was a full sentence. Then she does something that takes a long time, like hoist a new water jug into the cooler setup, before she presents a new sentence to continue off the old one. Capitalism has known Sara long enough to wait for the second sentence without interjecting—an interjection just drags the whole thing out even longer. "They want free ideas. Extra work they don't need to pay anybody for, concepts nobody can copyright, delivered to their door. You do it in the office, they own it, that's what it says in that horrible employee agreement we all had to sign before we got the first paycheque. And in return, what, someone gets a dinner bone? Genius. For less than a grand, everybody who works here throws their best ideas forward. Then they pull names out of a hat probably, you get a steak in return for your best idea if you win, and if you lose you get nothing at all for it. No matter what, they've got everyone's best off-the-clock work in hand for less than pennies on the dollar."

Capitalism nods. Sara's right, of course. Still, he hungers to win. This is his flaw, he knows. His weakness. He is one of those poor suckers who will enter the contest, even though he knows it is too good to be true, that promises of promotions are not even that, not even promises, just rumours. Rumours fed by the company but just rumours, to be later denied. Capitalism knows all this, understands it, intuits that Sara has hit the proverbial nail on its head with her insubordinate hammer, but Capitalism cannot act on this knowledge. He can only act on his hunger.

And so, Capitalism nods, tells Sara she's right, she's got their number, crushes the empty Starbucks cup he has been carrying all morning just so nobody offers him some terrible hipster coffee. Even as he's walking away, he's cycling through possible ideas.

▼

CAPITALISM SPENDS THE REST of the morning in his office crumpling paper. A yellow legal pad in front of him on a cleared-off desk. Yes, Capitalism has an office, an office with a door. Capitalism rose fast but is still in middle management. Fast to others, slow to him. Capitalism hungers, has no patience. Wants to win that contest. Wants to skip ahead. The faster his rise, the further he shall rise. This is what Capitalism believes. If his hunger does not undo him in some way.

Capitalism worries often about that hunger. About never being satisfied. When his children come home with As, he wants to see A-pluses. When they come home with A-pluses, he wants to know if there were bonus questions, if they could maybe skip a grade. Once his wife tried to strip for him, slow and sexy, but he couldn't wait that long. He took her halfway through, which pleased her but upset him. Why couldn't Capitalism wait for the show to finish? Why can't Capitalism get to the end of a movie without googling spoilers on his phone?

Capitalism promises himself that he won't do that this time. He will sit here in this office until he has devised the perfect proposal. His desk is bare except for the one yellow pad, everything else tumbled into drawers or onto the floor. He told his secretary to hold all calls, just like in a movie. And just like in a different kind of movie, she asked if that meant they were going to have some fun today. But he has no time for that.

Today he must focus. Capitalism will come up with the best idea, will crush the competition, win the contest. He will slice steak in front of the CEO. His knife-handling second only to his conversational skills, Capitalism will impress the CEO and rocket up the ladder, or whatever the better metaphor would be, rocket into orbit? He will shatter all glass ceilings, vibrating as fast as he can, travelling as far as he can. He will keep moving upward. The company building has ninety-seven floors, the tallest building in the city, sixteenth tallest in the world. The CEO in a penthouse on top. For all this talk of "flattening the pyramid" and "horizontal management," the company is a vertical hierarchy, and everyone knows it. Your floor is your rank. They are old-school in that sense.

Capitalism's office is on floor 42, and he intends to double that by the time the smoke from this contest has cleared.

But to do that he needs an idea.

The crumpled yellow paper balls pile up. Day clocks out and night starts its shift. Capitalism ignores his wife's texts and his secretary's too. Until finally, though he never tires, Capitalism closes his eyes at his desk and stops moving, defeated.

▼

ON TUESDAY, CAPITALISM TRIES AGAIN. And Wednesday. And Thursday. The yellow paper balls continue to pile up. His secretary tries to take them away, but Capitalism refuses. He wants his failure in his face, to be punished like a dog that made a mess. Keep holding his calls. Keep his wife at home. Delivery for all of his meals. Tomorrow is Friday, when the contest ends, and he hasn't got one proposal worth anything.

Surely, his secretary asks, surely he's being too hard on himself. He needs a break. She could be his break. She smiles and winks again, but he throws his Thai takeout at her. She quits, not needing this shit. Says she'd call his wife if she thought he'd even care. He doesn't. He cares only for silence. About focus.

He knows the problem: his hunger. He can't stay on one track long enough to see it through. He can't move to the end of the idea, can't even flesh it out to fill a single page before dissatisfaction fills him and he flits to another idea, hoping this new one will sate him. He feels like a crow, flashing on shiny things, but even as he berates himself for his inattention, his movement, he knows at the same time that this movement is his strength, this inattention keeps him searching for the right idea, keeps him from settling like the others will settle.

He will find the right idea. He will find it.

But the deadline looms. The deadline stalks him. Comes closer, closer. It caught his scent in the wind and is coming closer now, coming in for the kill.

▼

FRIDAY AFTERNOON HE'S AWOKEN by his secretary coming back, having realized she cares more about the money than about him, which was always their connection. He passed out early that morning, exhausted for the first time in his life. Slept without disturbance because in her rage she finally left him alone like he demanded, the one time she fucking listened to him. Then she returned to find him collapsed on the floor atop a cushion of crumpled yellow paper. Now the deadline has come.

She has come for the final idea, to deliver it, but he has nothing. On the corner of his desk sits a crisp white sheet of company letterhead, right beside the scrunched-up yellow pads, a perfect ivory sheet of paper ready to receive his great idea, the one he hasn't had.

146

Capitalism's secretary gives him a sad-puppy look, which shatters whatever his chest holds in place of a heart. "I'm sorry." That horrible look. "There's no more time. I need to give them something."

"Just ten more minutes."

"The deadline is strict. They made a point of telling me."

He nods, defeated, panicked. He grabs the crisp white sheet and takes his pen, not the printer but his pen scrawls an idea across the page. He doesn't even know what the idea is until he writes it down.

When he looks at it, it shocks him. When he hands it to his secretary, her eyes go wide.

"Are you sure you want me to—"

"Just go, hand it in quick. Before I have time to think."

She swallows. Looks at the paper again. Looks up at him, terrified. But then she nods, small, quiet, and hurries away, her red heels tapping down the hall.

▼

OF COURSE, CAPITALISM WINS THE CONTEST. It is what he is meant to do. He buys a new suit for dinner with the CEO. He researches the menu, plans what he will eat (not steak after all, but wild boar) and spends a full day shopping for ties. He settles on a flashy one that features a crazed art deco Tutankhamen, to show that he still believes in pyramids.

The evening arrives.

Capitalism also arrives, and the restaurant looks closed, the door locked. He just stands there for a moment, stunned, but then the door opens and a handler waves him inside. She explains that the company paid the restaurant to close tonight and pare down to a skeleton crew. Only the chef and cooks are here, the wait staff are gone and replaced by company men. The CEO and Capitalism will dine in private, without anyone to overhear their conversation.

She drops Capitalism at his table, where he waits for the CEO. He doesn't know what to do with his hands. He sets them on his knees and studies the tablecloth, its soft lines arcing like brainwaves. He begins to doubt his tie.

Then the CEO arrives.

Handlers flank him like geese in a V. He beelines for Capitalism, who rises. Shakes hands with a crushing grip, but Capitalism has prepared for this and matches the force. The CEO smirks, one side of his mouth lifting and his eyes dancing. He sits, and Capitalism follows, lowering just a moment after.

They are quiet. The CEO stares at Capitalism, hands confidently flexing while his wrists rest on the table. The geese hover behind him. The CEO shoos them with a wave and they scatter.

"So." The CEO reaches into his front pocket and pulls out a folded piece of paper. He unfolds it in front of Capitalism. Capitalism recognizes this paper, of course. It's the proposal he submitted. The scrawl he dashed off in his office, under duress, with no time. "Pen was a nice touch." The CEO lays the paper down on the table, smooths it out with his confident hands.

Capitalism's proposal consists of a single sentence, ungrammatical and incomplete: *Kidnap other CEOs line them up in the alley cut their throats one by one the others will see*

The CEO smirks again and runs his fingers over the final words. "'The others will see.'"

Capitalism does not know what to say, so he doesn't say anything. He sips his water.

The CEO gulps some water as well, not to be outdone. He swallows and smiles. "The St. Valentine's Day Massacre."

One of the geese returns, bearing a bottle of champagne, uncorking it as he walks. Fills their glasses while the CEO talks. "Everyone knows now that Al 'Scarface' Capone ordered those killings. Everyone knew then. All of America knew. But, officially, the crime was never solved."

"Some historians don't think so," Capitalism says. "They point out that the rivalry with Bugs Moran wasn't that strong at the time. Think maybe it was payback for this one firefighter that had been killed, family and friends doing some vigilante justice."

The CEO waves it away. He taps the paper in front of him. "Stop the shit." He downs the champagne, rises to leave. "Pack your office." The geese flock back to flank him as he wipes his mouth. Before he turns away, his eyes drop slightly. "Nice tie."

▼

FOR A MOMENT, he thinks he's been fired. But no. Capitalism rises, and the company rises.

He climbs, floor by floor, proposal by proposal, and as their stock climbs and climbs he rockets his way, month by month, to the top. Near the top. By the time they purchase Apple, Capitalism is working directly under the CEO, in a special office under the penthouse suite where the CEO lives and works, a massive $17 million condo-office combination.

They take a business lunch together each day in a small dining room that doubles as a boardroom, to go over the morning and plan the rest of the day. Capitalism hardly sees his wife anymore—but don't feel sorry for her, that's what you sign up for when you marry Capitalism. His kids have adjusted well also, although he has a special savings account set aside to fund future therapy. His dog he's moved into the office suite for company.

As Capitalism waits in the dining boardroom for the CEO to arrive, he watches that dog through the glass doors. The dog shuttles down the hall toward him, seeing him through the glass. But as the dog nears the glass door, he notices it, sees it's closed, that even though it looks like nothing stands between them, Capitalism is inaccessible.

The dog's stricken with sudden disappointment, but it's learned not to scratch for entry. The dog knows Capitalism sees it, and knows he will not let the dog in. The dog wobbles as it changes directions, a bit unsure where to go now that its trajectory has stopped. Then it shuttles off down a turn in the hall.

Capitalism watches all this, thinks about the dog. His dog he never named, the dog whose sex he's never known. The dog he nevertheless chose for company over his family, because it has learned to take what it is given, to be happy with what it gets. Because it took to training well and never barks and does not beg.

What will the dog do now? wonders Capitalism. *And what will I do?* The CEO is late, as he often is, and he may not come, as he sometimes does not. *So what will I do?*

He looks at the glass doors for a long time.

▼

CAPITALISM HAS KOBE STEAK, served blue, without the CEO. He likes his steak with no sauce, no sides, not even wine, just water and meat. He knows some people add salt, but salt is for the weak. When Capitalism finishes the meal, he's still hungry. He's always hungry, even after he just ate.

He used to think this hunger a weakness. As he rises from his meal, he loosens his tie, that same Tutankhamen tie. Then takes it off. "The day is done." He speaks to the air, to the birds flashing past outside, to the sky. He loops off his belt also. He unbuttons his cuffs, undoes his shirt. He starts to strip.

He used to think this hunger a flaw. But when he won that contest, when he rose and rose and rose, he realized his mistake. The hunger is not weakness. The hunger is strength, his great weapon.

Naked, he strides from the room, gathering the steak knife as he goes.

Capitalism enters the elevator, punches the code for the CEO's suite. Naked, still holding the long, serrated blade. The elevator doors close, hold shut, then open, all soundlessly. And Capitalism strides, also soundless, into the penthouse.

He angles down the hall, slicing straight to the bedroom, where he can hear the CEO grunting, thrashing in the middle of rough sex. Capitalism steps naked into the bedroom where the CEO is hammering himself into a large woman, while another man, possibly her husband, looks on.

The room has only a moment to register his presence before Capitalism sinks the beautiful knife into the CEO's throat and saws it down and across.

The CEO's hot blood spurts then gushes while the others rush away from him, away from the horror, although they don't scream, nobody screams and the whole scene unfolds in an eerie silence. A calm, strange quiet, broken in jagged moments by blood splattering the marble tile and flesh slapping as it either flees or falls.

▼

CAPITALISM LEAVES THE bedroom without even bothering to watch the CEO bleed out. Leaves the knife in him, its purpose served. Clothed only in blood, Capitalism strolls across the room, steps onto the balcony.

151

Looks out over his city. No buildings are taller. No balconies higher than this. He tastes the thin air. He draws the sky into his lungs.

Capitalism grasps the railing, in a grip so strong it twists the metal. He pulls himself up, to sit on the rail, legs swinging down into mist.

He lets himself fall. He falls. Capitalism rushes to the ground. The ants below lift their heads to watch. They grow as they take him in. The eager pavement speeds nearer and nearer.

He's not worried. Why should he worry? This fall means nothing. He will not break one bone. It's the earth that will break, when he hits it. When his body craters the city, and the whole world wraps around his skin.

THE WAR WITH THE DEAD

EARLY IN THE HISTORY of the war with the dead, the living invented their gods. Soon these gods were dead. Some rose again in doomed defiance, but at best were brittle zombies. Those the living had imagined as their heroes, the names they thought would secure immortality, soon joined the ranks of the dead.

This is the history of the war with the dead. Every weapon the living invent turns upon them. Yet they keep inventing new gods, new heroes, new weapons. Each new thing arising in response to the death of the old. Yet for the dead, there is no newness, no age. Only death, a gift held aloft, which the living first refuse and then reach for.

Which will one day be given. Where all gods one day go. In which all heroes, all weapons, are enfolded. To which all is destined from birth.

▼

YET THE LIVING resist. They drag their resistance into the future, where they die, and join the ranks of the dead. They turn on one another in their fury, when they do not willingly turn traitor, marching into the past in defeat.

The great battleground in the war with the dead is time. The dead now hold the past. The living hold the present, though the dead maintain their territories. The future is the realm still in dispute. As the future draws into the present, it is colonized by the living, and then ceded to the dead.

Each secure in their stronghold, the living and the dead both turn their faces to the future. Their weapons turn with them. What complicates the battle is that neither may enter the territory they dispute, only cast things there—their weapons, their resistance, their desire. They set events in motion, chain them forward.

The living set explosives in the present, sending explosions into the past. In this way, they plan to take the future. The dead, by contrast, revel in these explosions. They glory in ruins, create objects from the rubble. They launch these into the future, and laugh when the living drag them down into the present. In this way, the dead wage war.

▼

THE DEAD CREATE dead objects from once-living objects. These objects do not interest the dead. The dead do not know their names. They return them to the living, after radiating them with time. The living should resist them, should destroy them, cast them back into the past. But they do not. Instead, they treasure them and seek their forgotten names.

The living seek to revive these objects, not knowing the mistake of this, not understanding the nature of death. Unknown objects, archaeological objects, these missives from dead cultures constitute and embody a threat. Dead objects, which are pure objects—without names, without utility for the living—are the greatest possible threat to present concepts, present order.

154

Testaments to a world that was once, but is no longer. The presence of these dead objects threatens the living, threatens to unravel their world. To void its uniqueness, its consistency. Kill its future. This is why the living put ancient vases in museums rather than destroying them or putting them to use. Like all dead objects, they must be isolated and categorized, castrated. The threat they pose must be removed.

▼

ART, LIKE ALL else, is a weapon employed by both the living and the dead. The living use art to comprehend dead objects, to imbue them with a living mystery, and in this way exorcise the demons that the dead trapped in these objects. The dead laugh. The dead use art like any other dead object. They take it from the living, draw it into the past, and cast it forward to the future, so that it ends up in the present to destroy.

Thus the art of the living becomes the hoard of the dead, alien documents, incomprehensible. The dead imbue these things with death, and then return them to the living. The living, not understanding the nature of art, and of death, make the same mistake that they make when approaching all dead objects. They attempt to enliven them, to incorporate them into the realm of the living. They study, interpret, analyze, over-interpret, proclaim the undying, universal, classical nature of the dead's art.

All of these actions are designed to defuse this art, to dampen its disruptive power. To cut the red wire, stop the bomb. But the bomb has already gone off. Life crosses into its continuing explosion.

▼

FOR THE LIVING, immortality means to walk through then return from the land of the dead, so they build their art on the models they have drawn from the dead. They then cast this art into the past. The dead recreate it for the future. To destroy the future, to disrupt the present. The dead create with violence, to do violence, so craft art as they craft all things—with pleasure.

The future is filled with objects, like art, with traps the dead have laid. The art of the dead, like all of its objects, bears no message. Its presence is its message, its violence. The dead reshape the art of the living so that, after it is returned, its shapes might resist the living's attempts to understand and defuse them.

What the living do not understand, when they look to the future, is that it may not yet belong to the dead, but it can never belong to them. The future will not be won, except by objects. Their weapons, whether skyscrapers or poems, will be the true victors of this war.

▼

THE LIVING SHALL NEVER DEFEAT US. We shall enfold the sun in our arms. Already the stars come to us, one by one, dwindling.

We the dead shall defeat our unborn. They shall fall gentle to the earth from ancient storms.

156

THE OCEAN FROZEN, Aleya does the one thing she can do. She steps upon its surface. Steps over the book, onto the frozen sea.

This is wrong, she thinks. *The book should be an axe.* The Kafka quote comes to her, she speaks it into the night: "I think we ought to read only the kind of books that wound and stab us. If the book we're reading doesn't wake us up with a blow on the head, what are we reading it for? So that it will make us happy...? Good Lord, we would be happy precisely if we had no books, and the kind of books that make us happy are the kind we could write ourselves if we had to."

As she speaks, her feet move over the ice. Her socks soak, her feet chill. "But we need the books that affect us like a disaster, that grieve us deeply, like the death of someone we loved more than ourselves, like being banished into forests far from everyone, like a suicide."

Is this her suicide? In the distance, far away, she sees a glow. She moves toward it.

"A book must be the axe for the frozen sea inside us. That is my belief." *Is* it her belief? Was it even Kafka's? Or just a thing to write? Something to say?

But her book lies frozen in the sea. Not an axe but the source of its ice. And the sea not in her, but beneath her. And its words wrapping her like the night.

THE PALACE OF ICE

IN HER DREAMS, Sara glides through long corridors, in endless motion, lone occupant of the tremendous palace of ice. Her dress is long, adorned with flawless stones, diamonds as clear and as cold as the palace walls. Trailing on the floor, the dress obscures her feet, which are bare, and by taking tiny steps and maintaining a careful, uniform speed, she is able to give the illusion that she is not walking at all, but sliding or perhaps floating down these endless, impossible halls.

There is no one around to observe this motion but her dreaming self, who watches with approval as the dream-Sara moves, unblinking, through the palace. In this dream, in all of her dreams now, there are no rooms in the palace, only criss-crossing corridors. Though they would appear identical to most, she is able to tell them apart by slight differences in light.

There are so many of these corridors that, in all of her dreams, Sara has never traversed the same one twice.

The sun is not visible here, its brightness diffused by the ice in such a way that the walls, ceiling, and floor stand as the palace's source of illumination. The quality of the light changes as she moves throughout the palace, each stretch of ice holding and relinquishing new light.

There are no shadows. Light bathes her from all directions, and if there is darkness anywhere it dwells within her body.

▼

SINCE SARA READ about President Niyazov of Turkmenistan and his demented order to construct a palace of ice, "big and grand enough for 1,000 people," in his desert country, she hasn't wanted to eat. So she's forced herself. Every day after work she makes a point to try out a new restaurant. She can't just sit in a restaurant and not order. She doesn't eat much, but she eats.

Her ritual is ordering the fifth thing on the menu and the seventh thing on the menu, and putting a dab of Heinz 57 ketchup on the side of her plate. She brings the tiny ketchup bottle from home, where half the time it is the only thing in her fridge. She doesn't eat the ketchup, but the dab is part of the ritual, the red reminding her of blood, that food is life. She must remember that food is life.

But the food all tastes like death.

She picks at rigatoni and dreams of the palace of ice. She wonders if he built it. Niyazov built many incredible, tremendous, logic-defying things. A "neutrality monument"—a monument to neutrality!—with his statue at its peak. Rotating to always face the sun.

But did he build the palace of ice? She can't find confirmation of its construction online, just the same BBC article that he ordered its construction, again and again. She tried to contact its author, to ask for more information, but no reply. Not a surprise. The story from 2004, this already 2014. Only a decade later, but Niyazov is already dead.

▼

IN SARA'S DREAMS, her body is perfect. Wisp-thin. It slides through the palace of ice, through its endless corridors, wafting. The jewelled dress curling around her wiry frame, in a breeze that blows them both.

She wonders about the breeze. In the dreams, she never sees a door. She never sees a window. Just endless, translucent corridors. But the breeze constant. Perfumed, desert blossoms (her imagination of desert blossoms—petunias and roses, mixed, with an acrid undertone). Warm, a caress of fine silk.

It should melt the walls. It should but it doesn't. So should her skin. Her bare feet, at least, should leave streaks, dainty footprints. But they don't, don't even feel damp. She steps over the cool ice floor, wafted by a warm desert breeze.

Since the ice she contacts doesn't melt, her skin must be cold. She is always cold when she's awake, though in dreams she just feels nothing, numb. But must be colder than this floor, these walls.

▼

SHE'S LOSING WEIGHT. Forcing herself to eat, but still losing weight. Not enough. Not enough. She forces herself to order the full portions. She forces herself to order juice. She takes two hours to finish. She gags when she tastes the juice.

Her mother scolds her. "Not all this again."

No, she thinks, she says. *Not again. I am doing everything right.*

"Then why do you look so terrible? So terrible, so thin."

I am doing everything right. I am ordering at restaurants. I walk there and I walk home. I am intentional. I do not know what is happening.

"What always happens. Always, always, with you, Sara."

No, she thinks, she says. *No. I am eating. I am. Maybe the walking. Maybe I walk too much.* She begins to take the bus. Walking tires her anyway. She walks too much. Walks too much in her dreams, in her dreams, in her dreams.

She closes her eyes. Begins to nod off on the bus. In the palace and its endless corridors. In the palace of her frozen dreams.

▼

AT WORK SHE TAKES DICTATION. This is her job, to take dictation, something the computer could almost do by itself. But the boss likes her. Why does her boss like her? She doesn't understand, she never has.

Victoria looks away from Sara, out the glass wall, as she speaks, as Sara types. "Difficult decisions have to be made for the good of the company, the good of all." Sara rolls her eyes, and too late wonders if Victoria can see her eye rolls reflected in the window. If she does she doesn't say so, just continues. "You will be informed of these decisions in the weeks and months to come. Worry not about the consequences of these decisions. Everything will work out in the end, for a happier, healthier workplace. Read it back to me."

Read it back to me, Sara types, before backspacing over the sentence. Then reads the memo back to Victoria. As she reads, she wonders how Victoria is going to justify Sara's job in this new round of cutbacks. Sara certainly couldn't.

"I hate using all that passive voice. But that's the job." Victoria turns away from the window, to face Sara. "How's it going, Sara? You're looking thinner."

She stiffens and forces a smile. "Fine. Walking a lot more. They say the muscle weighs more, even if it looks like less."

She hopes she said that right. The way someone who worried about weight gain might say it, with a hint of *what-can-you-do?* in her voice. But probably it just seems like a non sequitur. She tries to change the subject. "Maybe you should avoid that odd phrasing of *Worry not*."

Victoria doesn't bite. "Yes, well. Don't walk your feet off." Victoria forces her own smile, and Sara sees now, sees that *this* is why she still has a job. Victoria *knows*. Victoria has been there and *knows*.

A wave of nausea rushes Sara, and intense stomach pain. From the sickening sympathy. She excuses herself and hides from Victoria in the bathroom through her lunch hour.

▼

THE DREAMS SHIFT. A subtle shift, and she doesn't notice it at first. The dress is shorter. She trails her diamond dress through the crystal corridors, the frozen halls, and with each turn down a different passageway the dress seems shorter. As if it were melting like the ice should melt. When she looks behind her (looks at herself looking behind her, in these strange dreams, where she floats outside of her body), she sees a trail of tiny diamonds, a thread of light winding through the palace labyrinth.

Soon the dress stops dragging over the floor. It still trails away, though, turn by turn. Soon it has come up to her ankles. But she has no ankles. Her numb feet wisped away.

Where the dress ends, her body ends also. She's walked her feet off after all.

▼

SHE CATCHES COLD, or maybe flu. Sick so she calls in sick. Victoria calls back in the early afternoon, after lunch with whichever loser from middle management she's planning to fire next. "How bad is it? Do you think you'll make it tomorrow?"

"I hope so." *Why don't you just ask?* Sara screams inside. *Just ask.* "But hard to say. A fever."

"Are you throwing up?"

She's surprised to hear Victoria so direct, so aggressive now. Is about to tell her to shut up, to back off, but remembers they are talking about something else. They are talking about her sickness. Maybe flu.

"I just have no energy. Can barely get myself out of bed." Too true and she doesn't want to be honest, not with Victoria, so adds a lie. "But went for groceries this morning anyway, just for some exercise."

"Hmm. Well. Feel better, okay?"

Fuck you. "Thanks. I'll try. And thanks for calling, you don't need to."

She reads in bed. Enough walking for now. Her legs so tired. She walks enough in her dreams. She doesn't eat. Feed a cold, starve a fever, like they say.

▼

WITH EACH DREAM NOW, the halls gain patterns. Their walls, once smooth and seamless, now etched with blooms. Swirls and spirals, elegant shapes, scratch across each surface. At first she thought them cracks, but as they blossomed and spread she realized they were adornments, tiny trails cut into the ice with invisible skates.

With each new dream they spread and thicken. From the middle of the walls to crawl over the ceilings and floors. They disturb her, because they prism the light. The dull, translucent glow gives way to thin, sharp rainbows.

She doesn't want these rainbows to touch her. As the palace of ice changes to grow more beautiful, she starts to feel unworthy. Out of her element. Her element is ice. As the palace turns to light, her dreams turn into nightmares. Soon she dreads the palace, dreads sleep.

▼

VICTORIA COMES TO SEE HER. Sara doesn't want to let her in, but doesn't have the strength to argue. So she doesn't argue, just sits and listens while Victoria talks, lectures. After a while Victoria leaves. The whole scene passes with such vagueness. Whatever Victoria says to her, whatever she says in response, begins to melt once it contacts the air.

▼

THERE'S A STORM IN THE PALACE, in its heart. The palace is a crystal formed around this storm. These epiphanies come with the clarity of dreams, where everything makes sense and everything is perfect. The diamonds that fall from her fading dress, the prismatic rainbows that torture her skin, the patterns etched over her walls.

She feared the storm, when she first suspected its truth. Now she seeks the storm in each dream, down every hall.

Sometimes she pauses in her seeking to discover herself dragging diamonds across the walls. She's the one making the patterns. She's the one unleashing prisms and light. She's never going to die and she's never going to go home.

▼

THIS IS HER DECISION. This is the decision she makes. She will live inside this dream. In her palace of ice. In the heart of its storm.

She will stand, as the palace stands, impossible, in this desert. Screaming her impossibility into the desert. The desert cannot reach her here. It sits impotent, still, silent, outside her walls.

Trapped there, trapped outside, in an endless expanse. Defeated, dreaming its own dreams, of water.

NARCISSUS

HE RAISED HIS FACE from the water to the mirror and saw his true reflection.

The scar below his left eye now in front of his right. The reflection's left eye was no longer the mirror inverse of his right, but a perfect replica of his left. As if he faced his same-scarred clone. Consider this, in your mind's own eye.

In that terrible eye with its own jagged scars.

▼

INVOLUNTARY, HIS LEFT hand rose to brush this scar. His reflection raised its own left hand (raised the hand on his right side) to its own cheek, its own scar. *His* reflection? The world was all doubt. It was no longer the world of physics and light.

A mirrored reflection became a true reflection and everything shattered but the mirror. The mirror remained, uncaring and indifferent, solid and eternal in a world of fragile shadows.

He stared at this mirror and willed himself not to blink. A blink too uncertain. If after blinking he no longer saw this, if the world resumed its old ways, then he would miss the miracle. And if, after blinking, he *still* saw this? If the world he knew did *not* return, what then? What could he do?

He felt pressure build in the base of his skull. His head buzzed with the crackle of synapses. His eyes watered as they flicked from point to point in the mirror's senseless body. He stood naked in the bathroom's flat light, exposed to the reflection's restless gaze. His eyes hurt, forced a blink. So he shut his eyes and held them closed for as long as he could bear.

▼

THEN OPENED HIS EYES, returning them to the mirror. He stared into his own eyes and winked, his left eye fluttering. In the mirror, in front of his right eye, the reflection's left fluttered.

He dropped his gaze, yanked the tap to blast cold water into the basin. He plugged the sink and closed the tap, pulled the cold water into his hot face.

He raised his face to the mirror again, and there it stood, his reflection, his pure reflection, a scar under its left cheek.

The basin dragged the water from his face in staccato drips. The sound echoed, a rattle like tin drums dying. Everything forgotten. He'd been preparing to—what? He'd been preparing but he was not prepared.

He raised his left hand again. And again, the reflection raised its left hand in perfect mimicry. There was nothing mocking, nothing sinister in the gesture. The reflection as awed as he. So this is what awe looked like. This boundless, holy terror.

▼

HIS NEXT THOUGHT, an idiot thought, was that maybe the mirror was broken. Defective. He sped from the bathroom.

The television was on, spouting noise, and he turned it off. He moved his face up to its blank screen. Static crackled fuzzy against his nose. Raising his right hand to his face now, to cover his right eye. Dull and dark though it was, the reflected eye before his left went black.

Then the kitchen. In every mixing bowl, in every knife. A perfect reflection, pure and true, without deference to physics. He threw everything to the floor once he'd seen the reflection inside. Frantic and crying now. The knives scraped one another and cut his bare feet as he trampled them in his rush around the kitchen, but he noticed neither the noise nor the blood.

▼

CONTAMINATION, THEN. What was wrong was wrong *here*. He shot through the apartment door, down the stairs, into the street. Naked, trailing bloody footprints.

It was morning and a young woman jogged by, blond and bobbing. She crossed the street instead of trying to help. He glanced her way but she offered no reflection, so his gaze moved on.

No cars were parked, though they passed. An office across the street with mirrored windows. He locked his gaze to it and raised his arms above his head.

The reflection raised its arms and it took a moment for him to realize he'd raised both arms. So he lowered one, and the reflection lowered one, on the opposite side.

It was not a dream. Eyes open and turned to this.

He stepped forth, still bleeding, into the street. Cars squealed and honked but he did not notice them. The blond jogger saw him coming toward her and ran. He strode toward the mirrored glass.

▼

HE WATCHED HIS REFLECTION APPROACH. As he shifted his weight, it shifted its own weight to accord. He reached the mirror and stopped. The morning a panic now, people yelling to offer help but afraid to approach.

He looked down at his hands. They looked fine but he knew that they were shattered. He knew that he was broken. These mirrors had broken him.

What could he do? Nothing, ever again. There was no safety. There were no guarantees. He put his hands on the mirror against his other hands. He put his face to the mirror and drowned.

AS WE ALL SHOULD LIE

WHATEVER HAPPENED TOOK PLACE in the night. When I awoke, when we all awoke, our backyards, once separated by thin fences, stood a full block apart. Divided by a large, empty lot and two thin streets.

I first saw this new block that had sprung from the ether when I went out to feed Einstein, stupidest of dogs. The invisible hands that reshaped the land had met in my back-yard just inside the fence. When they pulled apart to separate my once-neighbour Sarah from me, they dragged the once-common fence along with her. And from my now-fenceless backyard the dog had fled. As though from so tremendous a force there could be some banal escape.

I stepped out into the impossible street that ran where Sarah's yard had once lain. It supported me like a real street would. Already there were potholes. A car's horn jarred me back into the house.

In the kitchen I stared into an empty cup. Then the door-bell rang. Sarah. From across the new block. She told me she'd driven around it rather than walk across.

Then madness, a flood of people, conferences on back lawns, across remaining fences—talk, endless talk, and at the end of the day, at the end of it all, we still knew nothing, know nothing.

▼

CITY OFFICIALS GRUMBLED about whose problem this was, this impossible block. While they argued, they sent forth surveyors. Then fired them and sent forth more. When the second team came back with the same findings for which the first was fired, a chill settled into the city that even the record summer heat could not drive out.

The surveyors agreed that although this new block did take up space, it nevertheless did not alter the physical landscape outside of its immediate area. The block appeared between 3rd St. and 4th St., below 16th Ave. and above 15th Ave., but these streets stood unmoved. Nothing had been changed in the surrounding landscape, but somehow the block had been added—the empty block and its new framing streets, which connected to the aforementioned avenues as if having been there always.

And yet the block did not change the world around it. The streets remained straight, did not bulge.

There was just *more* in the city now, *more* between those streets than before. There was *more* and the *more* could be measured. Static and unchanging. Abiding by the physical laws of this universe, although its appearance and persistence stood in plain refutation of those laws.

A bubble—a rectangular, block-shaped bubble—had erupted in the fabric of space and *more* of the world had risen to fill it, without otherwise disturbing the surface of the (until now) ordinary world.

▼

DAZED AND PANICKED, City Hall responded with insane disavowal in true bureaucratic form. It named the new streets 3A and 4A and announced that, pending negative results of a test for radiation at the site, its real estate would be zoned residentially (in accordance with the surrounding area) and auctioned off.

Almost immediately, a fierce bidding war ensued, driving the property value of the now-named "Block A" up beyond meaning. While developers fought, and Calgary rushed to introduce a complex array of senseless bylaws, in a strange turn the property value of everything surrounding Block A plummeted. Nobody wanted to live near this philosophical disaster.

Only I remained after the first night. Everyone else sold, most to speculators who intended to hold the property while staying far away from their new "homes." The others in the neighbourhood stayed with friends, family, lovers, or in hotels until their sales went through. Sarah moved back in with her ex-husband.

I stayed in case Einstein returned. And every morning stepped out back into the nightmare. Before she left, Sarah begged me to come with her. She knew that I had no one, said that David wouldn't mind. Of course, he would have, but it didn't matter. I had to stay.

▼

SOON, CROWDS APPEARED. Tourists, first from across the city, but then from across the globe. As Block A became international news, a steady stream of travellers arrived, suitcases bursting with excitement. First, they circled the block. Then, after they'd built up enough courage, they stepped into the heart of its mystery. Then nothing. Despite its extraordi-

173

nary origins, Block A disappointed. A browning field of grass between two thin strips of pockmarked pavement.

The crowds dwindled, but interest in the block renewed when a mad development firm succeeded in securing the land rights. They brought in an avant-garde architect to design the new houses, which spilled over and twisted around one another, often sharing walls, almost sharing rooms, in some snaking perversion of suburbia that might have seemed natural in a parallel universe. Although these houses depressed the property values of the surrounding homes even further, they themselves demanded incredible prices.

For a while, then, Block A became home to wealthy eccentrics who were happy enough living there, although discouraged each morning to find they had not been whisked away by aliens or into an interdimensional portal during the night. In the middle of it all, my modest bungalow, ruining the view.

▼

SARAH STARTED CALLING. She never visited. She began reminiscing about the years we'd known each other, as if talking to a friend at my funeral. Then she started confessing secrets to me, as if I were a nameless listener on a help line. Then she called to say I scared her and she never called again.

▼

PEOPLE SPECULATED ON the cause of the block's appearance, the most popular conspiracy theories involving extraterrestrials or terrorists. A gaggle of scientists secured research grants to study the area, but learned nothing. Block A became a hot academic topic, but hundreds of doctoral theses and journal articles later, the world was no closer to any sensible answer to its quiet but unceasing question.

It became apparent that Block A intended to neither yield its mysteries nor produce new ones. Fascination dimmed and then diminished. The eccentrics moved away and let their twisted mansions rot.

Though Block A left an indelible mark upon the planet's skin, it did nothing to aggravate the wound. The world went on, dragging Block A with it. Assimilated into a universe that refused its possibility but had not denied its entry.

As for me, I wrote this down. But it was difficult and took many years. And yet so much is missing. The account so short, unremarkable—unrevealing.

▼

HOW IS IT THAT impossible things can appear, spit blank stares into our faces, and remain mute? Since we cannot look away, after some initial panic we make a show of ignoring them.

But I refuse to ignore this. I no longer sleep at night, surrounded by empty houses, with this chaos out the window at the foot of my bed. I no longer sleep, I just pretend.

I lie awake, as we all should lie, and await the coming of Block B.

WOLVES IN TRAINS

FEWER TREES IN THE COUNTRY NOW, fewer each day. The forests disappear. Fewer shadows on the ground. More light than ever before.

This light will burn out our eyes.

No packs anymore. No shadows where they might hide. This light was not made for hunting.

There are no other options. Nature, or something larger, has selected us.

▼

WOLVES IN THE GUISE OF TOURISTS. Moving.

Perfect actors. You thought you had killed us, driven us away, when you built your cities, buried the land beneath concrete. But. All along, there were wolves.

In the alleys. In grey coats. On your streets. Underneath. In the sewers. Beneath the stairs. Behind you.

Wherever shadows stretch and yawn. Where there is no fire.

Wolves.

▼

WOLVES DO NOT FLY. This is one of the laws of wolves.

But.

The children grow bold. Loll in clearings. Hunt near airports.

We worry. The young grow stronger, while we grow weaker. The way of all things is also the way of wolves.

They don't believe in limits. They think they will live forever.

▼

WOLVES DO NOT FLY. But. Though there is more food than the elders can remember, though we live in a time of plenty, our muscles ache for travel.

So. Wolves board trains. Passing over the land, passing fields where once there were forests. But we do not remember better days, do not yearn for lost times. Do not even look out the windows.

▼

WOLVES IN TRAINS. Moving. Passing through tunnels. Someone brushes you and the brakes *scream*.

Wolves are nomads. *You* are the one who desires a house, an apartment, a condo, a place to sleep, a place to work, a place to eat. Hotels, hostels, restaurants, video arcades, shopping malls, tents, cabins, cafés, parks, cardboard boxes in concrete alleys.

All places are all things. There is no difference between sleeping and working and eating. We pull into ourselves, tense, and are still. Until that moment when your step falters and we become motion.

▼

178

WE HAVE ONLY TWO EYES. One rests upon you and one upon our children.

But.

One day we will look into ourselves. And our children will tear out our throats.

I will not live to see the day, but one day wolves will fly.

▼

EVERY STORY IS TRUE, somewhere.

It does not matter that you do not believe.

ALEYA WALKS UNTIL her whole body numbs, until she no longer feels the cold, until she sees nothing but darkness. Over black ice, through night. But still that strange glow, from some distance. Diffuse, but as she walks, pulled onward by that invisible cord, the light begins to take on shape.

She walks for what must be days, although neither sun nor stars nor moon appear to guide her. Not a breeze blows to accompany her. Alone in the darkness, atop her frozen sea, Aleya walks toward some light.

As she moves closer, as it coalesces, she sees what it must be.

A star.

A star hovers over the ice, in the distance.

Aleya walks toward the star. It burns cold. A deep blue. The size of a skyscraper. Small, for a star. Roiling wisps of blue flame in the darkness above the ice.

Aleya steps toward the star. Glides numb across the sea. Toward its cold blue flame. She walks into its heart.

She's there already, of course. In its heart. Burning. A reflection she always dreaded. The other her.

An Aleya of ice meets an Aleya of fire. The frozen, numb statue steps into the heart of her star.

Where she cannot exist. She holds her hands out, to embrace herself. She offers her lips in a kiss.

She supernovas. The sea burns away. Light bursts out to scour away night. Her blue flame chases her darkness to the world's edge. Where it curls, nears extinction—but then she calls it back.

Aleya calls the night back. To the heart of her heart. Where she twines with herself. To become a black hole. The world ruined in the wake of her dying.

THE LIGHTNING OF POSSIBLE STORMS

I'LL STOP LYING to you now. She didn't read the other stories. She turned to this one first. Wouldn't you? In a book meant for her, she turned first to the title story.

Yes, Aleya turned first to this page, to the story that promised revelation. Then she read these sentences.

Then she screamed.

Dear reader, please don't think that I made her scream. Not on purpose. Even though I wrote this. I've stopped lying.

I've stopped lying and this is the truth.

▼

WHEN SHE CALMED down she read this. Aleya. Aleya, it's me. Your author, father, friend.

This time she didn't scream. She couldn't. Throat paralyzed. She dropped the book. Its pages spilled and bruised, bent back against the floor.

The book spoke its truth into the floorboards. Aleya huddled away from it, cold and terrified. Aleya, the book spoke, but she would not hear. Aleya, don't be afraid.

I write always for you. Write you stories as you serve me tea. Even though you don't exist. Write you into existence.

Put into you what I hate in me. So that I could forgive you. Could love you for the flaws that I fear.

I write to release you. From the frozen sea in you. This story, your axe.

I know that darkness, that ocean, its ice.

I know the night, know that numbness, know terror.

I look up for the stars, but just see darkness. I wish to be a star like you. When I was young, I found a dead bird. In the yard, face down under a tree. I thought that it still moved. Hopeful, I reached for it, a gentle nudge. It fell apart beneath my fingers, its false movement the slow roil of maggots.

I've been old ever since. One wormed through my fingertips, into my heart. I feel it move through me, feel it eating always. One day it will burst through my eyes.

Aleya, please help me. I don't know how to be who I am. I don't know how to say what I want. I need you but you are never here. I don't know how to live in this world.

▼

BUT ALEYA ISN'T reading now. She's burning instead. She's holding herself. She's a star.

WITH EVERYONE GONE, the books become her company. Aleya takes to entering strange homes. She wanders each evening, through a city abandoned to snow, until she finds an unlocked door. Stumbles through the darkness of the empty home until she finds a bed. Collapses, draws its strange covers over her.

When she wakes, when the sun wakes her, she follows the daylight, explores each new place. Through all this change, she has found it helpful to keep a routine. Slow, meditative breathing in bed, until she almost drifts back to sleep. Then she rises to the shock of the new room, but to control her disorientation she focuses on finding a book. Many people keep at least one book near the bed, a novel or a notebook. Often a diary. She takes the book into the kitchen.

That's the next part of her routine. She finds the kitchen, finds the coffee, makes herself breakfast while still holding the book. Everyone has coffee. Everyone has fake food that will not spoil. To boil the water, and cook, she builds a small fire in the sink.

She reads while she eats breakfast, so that she can hear the book's voice in her head as she begins her day. This is her world now. Empty and silent, its people erased. Whisked away, like a Rapture, to leave her alone.

She only meets others in books now. Voices droning from beyond oblivion about lost lives. The world outside just soft snow and blinding sky. The world inside a chain of strange rooms. After breakfast she reads until she finishes each book, then lays it in the fire inside the sink.

Since realizing she's a fictional character, she feels this is her duty. How many others writhe, like her, inside their books? How many frozen in these cold, dead worlds? This is her duty. To bring endings. To feed flames.

▼

ONE DAY SHE AWAKES in a king-sized bed, in an immaculate room. The bed grey and the room blue. The room expansive but empty, aside from the bed and a nightstand with a few books. Its starkness alarms Aleya—it does not seem like a real room. It seems like a stage, filled with props. No one could have lived here.

She opens the drawers of the nightstand: nothing. The books stacked in a too-neat pile: *The Castle* by Kafka, *Staying Connected to Your Teenager* by Michael Riera, and *The Monster at the End of This Book* by Jon Stone and Mike Smollin, the Grover picture book. A bizarre collection—who has a baby and a teen and a desire for Kafka, all at once?

Behind this pile of books, lying in wait, a smaller book. Beige, a notebook about the size of her hand. Large looping spirals for binding. Its cover mimics a library card, stamped full of dates.

Books to Check Out: A Journal. She turns to the back cover. In the centre of the beige field is a small white rectangle, and a quote: *"Read in order to live."* Gustave Flaubert 1867.

So, what if you want to die? She flips to the front and then opens the notebook.

On the left, a nameplate: *This Book Belongs to Jonathan Ball*. Of course. Her author. Aleya found his home, finally, or at least some fictional version. His name in neat blue pen, not his own messy scrawl. The book a gift.

Who was this man, this monster? What was he pretending to be? With a stroke of his pen he ended her world.

Aleya flips through the rest of the notebook—a list of books and movies, pencilled in then crossed out. Some she recognizes, some she does not. What was the point? Why had he led her here? Why leave this book for her? As a taunt?

I am his child also, Aleya thinks. What did he owe her, then? What did an author owe his character? Later that day, crossing the ice of the dead river, the answer comes to her. *He owes me the world*, she thinks. *I am his child, and he owes me the world.*

So here is the world.

▼

SHE WILL WRITE A POEM, Aleya decides. She has never written poetry before, not even in high school—always doodled instead, sad robots and broken hearts. Today, though, she needs a poem. Aleya knows this as she knows her name, feels its rightness. She will write a poem for the world, for its death. Write her way out.

She must learn to die as well.

Aleya finds a folding bamboo table and chair huddled into the breakfast nook of her author's house. She drags the bamboo set out onto the river's ice, midway across. She faces the chair away from the house, so she can look across to the other shore, to its forest. The unnatural snow came after the supernova, after the ocean disappeared and the city returned, at the height of summer. All the green leaves had flash-frozen on the trees. Then the snow's weight caused them to drop off. Across the ice now, a verdant shore. With trees like dark, skeletal fingers stretching up from fallen skin.

Aleya builds her fire in the sink and boils her coffee. But then, breaking the ritual, she takes her coffee to the river, to her makeshift office, and sets to work.

She stirs the coffee with her pen to keep the ink from freezing. Bundles in furs, hunches over, mars the flat field of the river's snow. Flips to the back pages of the beige notebook. Aleya has always written in notebooks starting from the back and moving to the front. That way, if someone found one and flipped it open, they would think it blank. She doubts now that she ever fooled anyone, but the child mind that devised this considered it a perfect plan.

Now, of course, there is no one left to look. No one to hide her words from. No one to read her poem.

She will write the poem anyway. Poems do not need readers, she decides. But why not? What are poems?

Poems are graves, she writes. Considers this. Then crosses it out. *A poem is a grave*. A line through that also.

This poem is a grave

Aleya can't say she likes that, not really, but it seems more precise. She doesn't cross it out.

This pen is a shovel
I am digging

Aleya doesn't know where she is going, but she goes on. She lets the words lead her.

I will dig through this page

Then I'll dig through this desk
Then dig into the snow
Then into the river
Through its ice, through dark water

Aleya thinks about the river. Are there fish there, below the ice? There are no birds in the sky. She has not seen any animals in the weeks since the world ended, no tracks since the snow fell.

I will dig into the riverbed
Through mud then clay then stone
Into the earth, into its burning heart

She isn't much of a wordsmith, she muses. The burning heart is a cliché—or maybe it isn't, given that the earth has a molten core? Probably still a cliché. But what does it matter? No one is left to judge her anyway.

Why is she writing? The poem seems pointless. She should stop.

But no. From her years at the tea shop, serving writers, listening to their babble, she knows. You can't stop. You have to keep going. You have to drag the words, drag their weight, until they gain enough momentum to move by themselves, until they start to outpace you. Until they run ahead.

Aleya looks across the river. New snow has started to fall. Someday white will blanket the bright jade.

I will have to keep digging, even then
I need a grave to hold the world

I need a grave to hold myself
I need this poem
Need it to hold me

We need each other
We're not alone

ABOUT THE AUTHOR

I DECIDED TO WRITE AN AUTOBIOGRAPHY. To prepare for the task, I tried to look the word up in my dictionary, but could find no mention of such a thing. Pages have been torn out of the book, others have rotted, and the day has yet to come when the tome offers even the slightest aid. Yet I keep it on my desk, ready for that day.

I know what an autobiography is, of course. Still, it is nice to have a thing defined for you, rather than defining it yourself. Best to look to others for guidance. Nobody likes someone who is antisocial. And everybody wants to be liked, though perhaps not loved. No, loved as well, though perhaps in strange ways.

"What does a life amount to?" you might ask. "Mere words," my autobiography might respond. Mere words. Should that sentence be followed by a question mark instead of a period? Well, how am I to know?

▼

I HAVE BEEN READING and rereading my books. Like good books, they are loved. I just reread Yeats and found a line in the poem

"Meru" that would make a great epigraph for my autobiography: "His glory and his monuments are gone."

My autobiography continues to elude me. It is a day later, though to read this you would not realize that, and indeed have no way of knowing if it's true. All I can think of is stories, and nothing from my own life will stay in my head for long.

Yesterday, I thought about a story I began writing over a decade ago, which I haven't thought about for years. In it, a man falls from the CN Tower. I visited the CN Tower and bought a postcard there, which is what inspired the story. When the man falls, nobody sees him except for a young boy, who watches as the man falls not *to*, but *through* the pavement. In his wake lies a stamped postcard, which the dutiful child drops into a mailbox. Years later, as a man, the child is not at all surprised to discover the postcard amongst that day's mail.

What did the postcard say? Well, I haven't written that part yet. Perhaps it will be something wise but heartbreaking, some comment on events in the boy's life between the time of mailing and the time of receiving the card. An affirmation of some choice perhaps, long brooded over and half-regretted.

That seems a bit precious though, and I don't think I'll go down that route, though I am not sure where else I might go. In fact, the whole thing seems too precious, and is perhaps better left unfinished, its redemption still possible.

I thought of that story yesterday, and of many other stories. Not a single one has anything to do with an autobiography, and I include this anecdote only for amusement's sake.

▼

I WENT FOR A WALK earlier today. Sometimes walking helps me to think of new stories, or to solve problems when I am struggling with a story. I need to think about something while walking. I thought I would be able to remember some interesting events in my life worth writing about, but all I could concentrate on was the cold.

I was torn between wishing that the snow would melt and wishing that more snow would fall. I always feel warmer when it snows, and it is more likely to snow than to melt, but I would rather the snow melted.

I should have walked longer than I did, but it was a cold day today. I will walk more tomorrow.

So now I have wasted another day, and am no further along in my quest to write an autobiography. How writers suffer. There is still a bit of time before bed, but my friends tell me to spend at least some small portion of the day shining my shoes, or doing something else society might consider useful.

▼

IT WAS A COLD DAY TODAY. There are many cold days in this city. It has been cold for a long time. There are many lights, but the lights do not help. I often feel colder to find myself standing under a street lamp, or outside a bar's neon glow.

On the corner near where I live, a tremendous structure announces the coming of a new pharmacy, another link in a chain of stores stretching across the whole world. The building is not yet begun, the sign advertises nothing, but still it stands, brighter than the stars, screaming its plastic message at the sky.

This is what we have chosen to build, instead of pyramids. Our glory and our monuments. You can close the book now.

ACKNOWLEDGEMENTS

THE TRUE DEDICATION of this book is to my children, Blake, Claire, and Jessie, the best distractions a dad could desire.

A number of these stories benefitted from advice or interactions with Patrick Allington, David Bergen, Keith Cadieux, Natalee Caple, Chris Ewart, Kaylen Hann, Bronwyn Haslam, Mandy Heyens, Jeremy Leipert, Suzette Mayr, Jay MillAr, Kathryn Mockler, Saleema Nawaz, Peter Norman, Glenys Osborne, Adam Petrash, Darren Ridgley, Virpi Salojärvi, William Neil Scott, Jessie Taylor, George Toles, Lindsey Wiebe, and Daniel Zomparelli. My deepest thanks to you all, and to all of my family and friends.

Many thanks to my Patreon supporters: Candice G. Ball, kevin mcpherson eckhoff, Reisha Hancox, Suzette Mayr (again!), Dan Twerdochlib, and Bryce Warnes. Much gratitude to Wren Brian, assistant extraordinaire, who keeps me sane.

▼

SPECIAL THANKS TO Stuart Ross, my editor for the press, and to Jay and Hazel MillAr, the heart of Book*hug, who published my first poetry book and now my first fiction collection.

▼

EARLIER VERSIONS OF THESE STORIES were published as follows:

"As We All Should Lie" appeared in *Atmosphere*, alongside its French translation.

"Capitalism" appeared in *Prairie Fire*.

"Costa Rican Green" appeared in *Etchings* and was short-listed for an Alberta Literary Award (the Patrick O'Hagan Award for Short Fiction).

"The Dark Part of the Sky" appeared in *A/Cross Sections: New Manitoba Writing*, edited by Andris Taskins and Katherine Bitney, and then later in *Etchings*.

"Judith" appeared in *Parallel Prairies*, edited by Adam Petrash and Darren Ridgley.

"The Nightmare Ballad of the Drunken Brand Identity with a Cameo by Shakespeare and a Title That Cannot Get Worse" appeared in *Joyland*.

"While You Sleep I Record Your Dreams" appeared in *The Rusty Toque*.

"Wolves in Trains" appeared in *filling Station*.

"The War with the Dead" appeared in *Poetry Is Dead*.

"Your Letter" appeared in *Etchings*.

▼

THE FIRST EPIGRAPH is taken from "The Masked Philosopher," from *The Essential Foucault* (New Press, 2003).

The second epigraph, which also appears in "About the Author," is from the poem "Meru" by William Butler Yeats (*Poetry*, December 1934).

Dan Brown does indeed say all of the things he says in "National Bestseller," in his Masterclass online video course, which is excellent.

The quotation from Milton in "Your Letter" is from the poem "On His Being Arrived to the Age of Twenty-Three" (1631).

The quotation from Slavoj Žižek is from the film *The Pervert's Guide to Cinema* (2006), written by Slavoj Žižek and directed by Sophie Fiennes.

"Judith" was written for *Machine of Death: A Collection of Stories About People Who Know How They Will Die*, edited by Ryan North, Matthew Bennardo, and David Malki, although it did not appear in that anthology. The story premise of the machine of death belongs to them.

The quotation in "George and Gracie" is taken from the second edition of Brian Greene's *The Elegant Universe* (Vintage, 2003).

The unattributed quotation on page 121 is from H.P. Lovecraft, "The Call of Cthulhu," *Weird Tales* (February 1928).

The quotation from Kafka is from his *Letters to Friends, Family and Editors* (trans. Richard Winston and Clara Winston).

▼

THIS BOOK WOULD NOT EXIST without the generous support of the Manitoba Arts Council and the Winnipeg Arts Council, or without you.

author photo: Michael Sanders

JONATHAN BALL is the author of eight books, including *Ex Machina, Clockfire,* and *The National Gallery.* He lives in Winnipeg and has won many awards, including a Manitoba Book Award for Most Promising Manitoba Writer. He hosts *Writing the Wrong Way,* the podcast for writers who strive to be bold and readers who crave something new. Visit him at www.jonathanball.com.

COLOPHON

Manufactured as the first edition of
The Lightning of Possible Storms
in the fall of 2020 by Book*hug Press

Edited for the press by Stuart Ross
Type + design by Ingrid Paulson

bookhugpress.ca